The Plate Shop

The Plate Shop

John Harvey
Illustrated by the author

www.hhousebooks.com

ISBN: 978-1-910688-88-5
Cover design by Ken Dawson Creative Covers
Typeset by Polgarus Studio

First published in the UK by Collins 1979
This edition 2021

Holland House Books
Holland House
47 Greenham Road
Newbury, Berkshire RG14 7HY
United Kingdom

www.hhousebooks.com

For Julietta

Foreword

Occasionally, driving, I'm stuck behind one of those large lorries the back-end of which consists of an enormous drum which, you presently notice, is very slowly turning round. It turns so the wet concrete inside it does not set on its way to the building site, and you can see, folded close to the mouth of the drum, the chute which will be lowered for the wet concrete to pour out. For me, however oddly, these lorries are the equivalent of those little yellow shell-shaped cakes which Marcel Proust might dip into a cup of tea, and find his childhood returning to him. Those giant slow drums bring back the several years in which, around the age of twenty, I worked in the local heavy engineering works.

Not that I was ever swarthy with oil and iron filings, or muscular from lifting sheet iron onto a drill-bed. My job was white-collar and unskilled. I had a desk in the office of the Time Study Scheme, which was just being introduced, where I cranked an old manual adding machine. I would add up the times assigned for different parts of a job, and take the sheaf of job-cards up to the Foreman. Or I went round the work-bays collecting time-cards from platers, welders, machinists, fitters, and back in the office I added up the times the jobs had taken. If there was a go-slow a plater might draw me into the depths of his bay, between the pin-ups and the sandwich boxes, and slip me a tight-folded knot of cards which showed, back in the office, they had still made an OK time for their bonus.

I worked there through my gap year. The atmosphere in the office was practical and friendly and I was glad to find I could work there again in my summer vacations from college. I had a connection because my grandfather had worked as a store-keeper there, another relative worked there later, and I followed events when a takeover threatened. 'Asset-stripping' was a term much heard at the time – the practice of buying a company not to develop it but to flog off whatever was saleable quickly. Closure and mass job-losses loomed, and also showed my young eyes the hard relationship between Money and Work in the world. When the idea took hold of making the factory a novel, it was clear this crisis must shape the story.

Through the long first year when I worked there, though, the factory mainly seemed a vigorous going concern. Shears squealed, hammers pounded. Huge tonnages of iron slid through the air; a sheet of steel, in a press, would flex like folded cardboard. Voices joked, talked football, swore or argued: at intervals 'Music While You Work' boomed indistinctly through the banging of iron. Elsewhere in the factory flames showed at the foundry-chimneys and when the man in huge goggles opened the hatch dazzling metal tributaries flowed into the moulds. At a height, in the General Offices, you saw the draughtsmen, in white shirts, at their slanted tables underneath the neon tubes. Eroticism smouldered in the passages round the typing pool and outside the apprentices would wolf-whistle to the messenger girls. As to Money and Power I can see like yesterday (it's not in the novel) the tall, black suited figure of Mr Ferguson, the General Manager, gravely conducting Major Leech, the Chair of the Directors, who did seem extremely old and brittle, down the length of the Plate Shop under the wary irreverent gaze of the platers. And in the acreage of yards outside the workshops the new big and small cement-mixers, plaster mixers and well-point drills, the batching plants and weigh hoppers and the truck-mixers themselves, multiplied countlessly, all shining in brilliant red, or yellow, or grass-green or sky-blue.

As the novel went through its drafts one figure slid centre-stage, the Foreman of the Plate Shop. He was the lynch-pin of the shop: the point of contact, or collision, between management and workforce. He could be peremptory but he also had ideas, and could originate improvements to the machines. He had, as they say, a big shadow, though in real life he was a short man, a bit hunched, who always wore a grey suit baggy from long use. I realized recently that I had included him in the old drawing of an accident that introduces my 'First Day' section. He is the man in the suit and cloth cap over to the right. And he had a wonderful name, too good for a realist novel: Joshua Slocomb Chard. My foreman has the surname Clyde, not so much to commemorate a great site of British industry, but because 'Clyde' is not too far from 'Chard'.

I always saw my Foreman as being a bigger-built man, with his jacket often more off than on: I was drawing partly on other foremen in the factory, but it's true my Foreman also has, in his mood and emotional temper, features of my father. On the other hand the relations of my foreman with his hard-of-seeing clerk Josh came straight from the life. And the real foreman was at odds with the Time Study in the way I describe. He had been in the job for years, and rightly saw the Time Study as interfering with his control of everything. Though he himself innovated he was out of tune with the larger changes going on around him, and it seemed to me afterwards that he had been like a factory – or an industry – on borrowed time, in person.

The people in the novel stand at different distances from the individuals I knew: none is an exact portrait, none a total fiction. There were also, in the workshop, big divisions like social ranks. At the bright end of the vast concrete and iron building, near the high open doors, the Fitters who assembled parts into whole machines were confident like an aristocracy from their skills and expertise. At the bottom of the heap were the labourers who lugged trolleys laden with steel from one work-bay to another. They were the butt of jokes, and as I visualize one of them now, it's clear to me that he was seriously depressed. I suppose that nowadays they would at least have fork-lift trucks to steer, not trolleys to lug.

The other, tiny disadvantaged group were the foreigners. There were not many – I remember especially an Italian and a Czech – and they were odd men out. While I was at the factory, there was an incident where 'race' came in which stayed with me and is prominent in the novel. It got no comment when *The Plate Shop* came out, but issues of foreignness and 'difference' have loomed larger since then. I even wonder whether the dire event of Brexit may have made this part of *The Plate Shop* topical.

But if a deafening oily factory workshop can at times be

full of shouting voices, disagreement, annoyance, the other side to all of that are the times when everyone there is swept along with fellow feeling. I've tried to give one instance in the last pages of the novel. Another is the swimming scene. But most I remember the tsunami of sympathy that took us all at the accident. Someone had been almost criminally careless, but alarm turned quickly to action, ladders came running as if they were legs, the platers swarmed up the rungs and hung out, heaving with crowbars and shoulders to lift a tonnage of iron, so the trapped apprentice with his crushed arm could be lowered. Afterwards I tried to draw the scene as I had seen it, coming in through the side door of the Plate Shop, and this now is my 'First Day' picture: I know it's not a Leonardo. Someone who saw it later said, 'Ah, you meant it like a Crucifixion'. I didn't, it's a concidence that the verticals work that way. But it is true that the barely conscious apprentice with his devastated arm was lowered and received with just that communal gentleness which you see in a good Deposition from the Cross: it's a human, not a theological thing. I suppose you could also say, in the big view, that the whole development of 'heavy' engineering was an iron crucifixion worldwide for the young men – and women, in the mills and mines – who had had little choice but to go and get hard jobs in factories.

When I sent *The Plate Shop* to publishers I was told that people don't want to read about work – at least in a factory: a newsroom, a police HQ, or the kitchen of a mansion is all right. I am grateful to Collins for taking it on, and giving it a good promotion so that it got good reviews: happily it was shortlisted for two prizes (the Hawthornden and Yorkshire Post) and won the David Higham Prize for the best first novel of the year. I was pleased when a positive report in the local

Suffolk press said that the factory, though unnamed in *The Plate Shop,* was known to be Garrett's works in Leiston, which suggested that the general description rang true (I had never then been to Leiston). It seemed to me that *The Plate Shop* had contributed to a television mini-series that came out in 1980: *Bull Week* was set in an engineering works and partly turned on the ill-treatment of an Eastern European workman there. An opening scene, where two workers, clocking in early, are struck by the beauty the factory can have, empty in the early morning, reminded me of my novel.

Visually, the original edition had a good but severe jacket, showing a corrugated iron door being locked up – or unlocked, a good ambiguity. The Fontana paperback showed a young worker like James Dean beside an older worker like Eric Porter in front of a building that looked, if anything, like a textile mill: Fontana explained that this combination should bring in a young urban public plus an older generation plus some L S Lowry enthusiasts. For my part, I had wanted the novel to have more pictures, because I had made some. The PhD research which I was doing at the time was on the illustrated serial novels of Dickens, Thackeray and others, and I meant to try something similar. Whether for their demerits, or because novels then never did have illustrations, my pictures were not used, and since the words are what matter for a novel, I don't regret this. But nor am I sorry that Holland House have decided to include some of the designs, quick drawings, and factory studies that I made at that time. At least they show the hold that the idea of 'The Factory' can take on one: factories do ask, dramatically, to be seen.

Pictures may stay when things depart. Without giving away the close of my plot, I can record that the factory I knew is now long gone. It was the Millars Machinery Company's works, at Bishops Stortford. It stood beside the main line south to Liverpool Street, and I used to see it when I took the train to London. Now the foundry chimneys, the giant humps of workshops, the square blocks of offices, have disappeared, leaving a wide low acreage of storage facilities. I am glad I had the chance to attempt my own sketch of what looks, at this distance, like the end of an era – of the 'Iron Age' of Britain, before Services took over.

John Harvey, Cambridge, 2021

First Day

1

The darkness gave way to a brown dusk, and a small face formed: the faded offering face of Marilyn Monroe. But all her gaze met, as the cold morning light advanced, was an enormous building, like an old hangar, choked to the roof with machinery. In front of her a rigid watching insect figure slowly condensed into a cap and goggles, and a leather apron, hung from a corner of iron. Nothing stirred; it only grew colder, and a sweat of dew came out on the cold steel plate. A thin mist crossed the receding humps and towers of grey machinery.

The light increased until the grimy windows of the workshop were white with sun, and the mist gathered to a horizontal blade, then disappeared. From dazzling points in the walls, pencils of light came in. Colours came out in the machines, which stood clear in all their different shapes: an upshooting wiry machine was all run and whip and gleam of tough silver threads; a square red casing stood rigid at attention, severe, burning in upright fire. Beneath a soaring tree of girders sprawled a long low humped and curved machine—deep–green, enormous—like a dangerous armour-plated creature asleep. In the girders above, a fat amber cable curled among the leads like a snake asleep among vines.

For two hours the sprinkled freckles of light inched down the girders and cowlings and went out on the concrete floor, while the machines faced each other. And still the faded lovely face of Marilyn Monroe, smiling, dimly sparkling, offered herself to the empty air, to the drills and presses, and to the enormous shape that had come clear in the centre of the Plate Shop: which just was, without joint, seam or interruption, a steel mountain, a huge smooth cone of iron.

There was a roar of cars, and a light ticking of free-wheeling bikes, then a paradeground tramp of boots moved round the walls. The side-doors were dragged open in a jagged scrape, and banged back echoing on the walls: and the first plater stood in the doorway, and shuddered as he came into the cold shop. The platers after him stood chatting in the entry, as they shook free of donkey-jackets and satchels.

The platers dispersed down the long chilly avenues, and a haggard, angular man began a slow, pausing climb up the sheer wall of the shop. Half-way to the roof he changed to a ladder with a protective cage round it: so he worked his way up like an ant or a fly, till he reached a wide bridge of machinery that spanned the shop. He clambered into a little cockpit slung under the crane; there was a thin quicksilver spinning and whirring of cogs up there, a thin wire of sound, and then in a soft large reverberation the entire machine began to slide gradually forward: the long claw, which hung down from the crane with the stretch and grab of an arm, swung slowly as it trailed in mid-air.

2

In one place, in the concrete cliff of the shop's wall, there was a dingy square wooden panel, and snap, it was banged up, and an old man leaned out as though he had been there all night. His eyes started from wide, dry, lashless lids: his skin was grainy and brittle: he was parched and arid like something bricked up in the wall breaking out at last. He glared down the shop, but when he saw the platers were all a long way off, he relaxed; he withdrew and then, with a fresh light in his old face, he just pottered about in his hole. The walls of his office seemed to be made of compressed bales of old rags, and there was a curious dim light, brightening upwards towards the top, as though the room were under water.

'Morning, Mr Petchey!' A plater came up to the hatch, nervously cheery, and the old man was instantly harassed with overwork. He only muttered 'Saville', and stuck a donkey-clip of tickets at the plater. While Saville filled them in, the old man leaned forward and watched him do it from close to, fiercely. He snatched the spidery tickets when they were done, and with one arm began with difficulty separating folded blue drawings from the crammed shelves. While he grumbled on the job, another plater arrived: tall, but stout all down his tallness, with a face all curves, humorous, clever and libidinous, and a bald pink head which he carried as though he had to show it off as something extraordinary in waxing and polishing. This plater did not know what nerves were, he came banging up to the hatch, crashed his fist down on the counter with a steelworker's disdain of wood, and bawled out 'Shop! Shop! The man, I say!' The nervous plater gasped, 'Careful, 'Lias, he's here!'

The old man slid to the counter smooth as if he moved on wheels, his dry eyelids hunched round the beads of his eyes; he muttered 'Trigg.' It seemed that the surname was the only word he could bring himself to say, as the all-in-one summary of his contempt.

'Morning, chief!' the new plater cried, and calmly wrote out his tickets. Then the two platers lounged across the counter, gazing offhand at the black glove hanging out of Petchey's right sleeve, a glove too small to hold a real hand. While Petchey worked with difficulty, they laboured to provoke him. 'Ah, Nutty, isn't he bonny at the crack of dawn! How do you do it, sunshine? Been at the Phyllo-san?' From the depths of the Drawing Stores, Petchey exploded, 'Clear off, hop it, go on, get out of it, you pair of mangy bleeding sods!' But the platers stayed lolling on the counter and he went on getting the drawings: they said the same things every morning, and all three felt braced. The routine row, first thing, was like starting the day with a small whisky.

Petchey came back to the counter, flung down the sheaf of drawings, and checked them off against the tickets; but now Trigg was fastidious and held up tattered oily drawings by one ear like dirty nappies. 'Oo, narsty drawing, I'm not having this.' The old man lost his temper and shouted he would go on strike, and bring the whole works to a standstill.

'Go on strike?!' the platers shouted. 'You can't go on strike!'

'Who says I can't go on strike?'

'Werl—it wouldn't be official, would it?'

'Wouldn't be official!' the old man repeated in cumbersome derision. Leaning out of the tight wooden frame, with the watery light brightening up the ragged shelves behind him, he shouted and swore at them, he would shut up shop and let them all go hang; there would be ructions, there would be hell to pay; he insisted on it till it seemed he wanted to do nothing so much as to brick up the tiny hatch there and then, and seal himself completely into the blank concrete wall.

The row they were making drew in a nearby plater: he came forward, holding a length of cable that trailed off into the shadows behind him, shouting at the old man, 'You'll be fucking lucky if you get time to strike, daddy-o. We all will.'

'Here, Lloyd, what do you mean?' the old man shouted. But the other two platers nodded seriously, at one with Lloyd, while he harangued them as though they disagreed. 'It's all cut and dried, all in the bag, you know that, don't you? Do you reckon we got months? Do you reckon we got weeks? We'll be bloody lucky if we've got a day!'

The platers nodded, and their eyes roved to the end of the shop and beyond as though what the bag had in it, was not only themselves, their machines, the factory, but the sunlight outside and everything it fell on. Lloyd shouted on, so that it seemed only his fear come real when suddenly he gasped and went down. A monster, a black snake, had got him: he rolled back and forth on the floor, and writhed like a man dancing, while the black coils whipped and spun round him. The serpent swerved and corkscrewed, and shook his arm furiously where it bit him; his white surprised face kept swinging into view. But the bald plater jumped down and grabbed the writhing fat black body, and gave it a great yank. As he jerked it back, the head darted round in mid-air to catch him, but he ducked, and it fell on the floor and lay quite dead there, completely still now, a red piece of skin at its minute jaw. Trigg traced the cable back to its end, and pulled it from the socket, explaining over his shoulder, 'The silly arse! He hadn't switched it off.'

Lloyd sat on the floor, dead white, holding up his hand and gazing at the small wound. Petchey chuckled from the hatch, 'Made him jump, did it?'

'You silly bugger!' Trigg kept saying to Lloyd, as he helped him to his feet.

3

Because the day would be hot, the wall-high doors at the end of the shop had been rolled back, and sunlight streamed in, catching corners of bright colour in the oily machinery, and dandling pale crescents of light on the undersides of the roof-girders. Not many machines were working yet; a sheet of plate riding out of the hand rolls curled up like a wood-shaving. The blade of the brake press came down, and with a sound like a deep breathing out, the two halves of metal plate flapped slowly up like rising wings. A loose-limbed plater, with a splay of fair hair like loose thatch, started to sing. He kept up opera and choir as hobbies, and Nutty Saville and 'Lias Trigg, returning with their drawings, made excruciated faces as they passed him, and walked on enjoying the snatches they got of the deep bass.

At the side door of the shop, Trigg paused. 'Eyes right, Nutty, here's Clyde!'

They waited while a middle-aged man walked into the workshop slowly: muscular, stout, with a large red impatient face. He was the foreman, and had an authority; he differed from everyone else in the shop by wearing a suit, though it was so bagged and bulged and worn to his shape that it looked more like his loose hide. From him, as he walked, came a muffled clank and chink as though he wore a loose suit of armour under his clothes: he had stuffed into his pockets every spanner, wrench, screwdriver and gauge that had ever come in handy in his rounds, and they made a jostling bulk of ironware.

'Morning, Mr Clyde,' Trigg and Saville murmured together.

Clyde gave them a nod so short and dry it was hardly more than a slight upward hitch of his face. Then he climbed a staircase against the wall, and went into a high office set over the doorway on four broad trunks of bolted girders. It looked like a short purblind watch-tower—the windows were so crusted with old grime that only a bleary browned glimmer seeped through, shifting as the foreman moved about inside. The platers knew his routine by heart. 'There he goes, old bugger,' 'Back he comes again,' they muttered, as the brown shadows coiled like trapped smoke in the dirty lantern.

The work-benches of Trigg and Saville were just past the foreman's office. '0i, oi, here's trouble,' Trigg said, as they arrived: across the gangway, a plater was arguing with a young man in a clean buff tunic, who stood fidgetting with a stopwatch, a biro and a small hardboard palette. It was the preamble to a time-study, and the plater, a lean serious man in glasses, was beside himself with annoyance.

'Good morning, Mr Dawson,' Trigg called to the plater, and then bawled at the time-studier, 'Morning, Barry darling, have you got a minute?'

Dawson smiled, and within his shapeless blue overalls, his wide shoulders went back like flexed wings. 'Hello, 'Lias! Morning, Nutty. D'you see they've set these buggers on to me again? Christ almighty, you'd think I'd earned a rest by now!' He complained earnestly across the gangway: they were timing him again for a job they had already timed once, only the week before.

'It's the price of fame, old mate,' Trigg replied, and Dawson, in modesty, cursed. He was the best plater in the shop, and the Time Study would never believe he was working as fast as he could; and it was true, he always did work slow when studied, out of loyalty to his mates. 'Time studiers,' he grumbled. 'They couldn't tell the time if you dropped Big Ben on them.'

'Don't be downhearted,' Trigg shouted. 'You've got a good friend up above. He's got a bloody grandstand view of this one.' He nodded up at the foreman's office, which stood just over them. The Time Study competed with Clyde in running the shop, and he loathed it more than the platers did.

'That's all I bleeding need,' Dawson said.

'Cheer up,' Trigg cried. 'Old Clyde, he'll chew up young Barry for elevenses and spit out the stopwatch.'

The three platers looked up, and watched the shadows stir in the high office; but Clyde stayed inside.

Dawson heaved round with a sigh and a shrug. 'Let's get the bloody thing done.' He went to the slaughter; the time-studier clicked his stopwatch in readiness; Trigg and Saville returned to their benches.

All the platers hated the Time Study: it gave them no rest and it gave them no peace. There was always lost time to be made up. Every hole gouged, every bar bent, every rivet gunned in; every job in the shop from dawn to dusk and dusk to dawn; all the seconds, hours, years, that had frolicked or slept or run away like water, were to be caught up with, measured, and nailed down on paper. Management's hope was that the ponderous iron-plated millstone of the shop's day, shuddering forward hour by grating hour, could be geared and oiled and made to whisk and spin, flinging out a fine flour of saved seconds that would turn to gold in mid-air,

11

clatter down musically, and accrue in rich piles on the floor.

Dawson placed a sheet of steel on his bench; the young time-studier said to him, 'OK, Mr Dawson, this is setting up.

But now Dawson kept digging out chalks and losing them, he kept finding odds and ends of unnecessary preparation, until he turned on Barry in a white glare of impatience. 'Well?'

'What is it?'

'For Christ's sake ! What do you want me to do first?'

'I don't know, Mr Dawson. What do you do first?'

Dawson shrugged, 'Well, it depends—what do you mean by first?'

Barry tore a sheet, and had to prepare another: every study of Dawson started the same way—he hulked there, helpless in awkwardness, like a great boy.

'Just do what you normally do, please, Mr Dawson, and forget I'm here.'

'That'll be easy.' Dawson began marking out the plates, but he flapped the drawing roughly and tore it, he banged the metal ruler down on the plate, and ground the chalk jerkily along it. And when the chalk snapped in his hand, he turned. 'Why should I stand it? I work well, don't I? Any complaints? Why should I be stood over, took down on paper, every fucking thing I do, every little bleeding atom? Am I on show?'

'I'm sorry, Mr Dawson. What do you think's best?'

Dawson wouldn't answer; none of his business.

Barry, fumbling, nearly dropped his stopwatch on the concrete. He put his palette and watch down on the bench. 'Let's call it off for today. What's the good?' He stood making as if to go, but he didn't go; he stood, white and rigid, and the humiliated, furious plater stood glaring at him. The stopwatch, with no hand to stop it, ticked louder in their ears than the raving machinery.

Dawson swung back. 'Bloody business . . . fucking . . . do what you like.' He resumed his work; but disjointedly, in rough fits and starts, with no sort of swing.

The times added up in a speckly trail down the sheets of ruled paper; but Barry only wondered, what earthly use would these times be?

A vibration passed through the shop in a kind of bush-telegraph: the foreman, Clyde, had come out on his balcony. The eyes of Trigg and Saville were suddenly caught in a spasmodic winking and gloating.

Dawson and the time-studier looked up at the large florid man in his bagged grey suit who was looking at them: motionless, solid, like an old works smouldering on the skyline.

After a long taking stock, Clyde descended, his boots clanging on the iron steps. When he started down the gangway, Barry froze.

Clyde, however, walked straight past: he had other affairs at present, and Barry watched after him as he walked deliberately down his shop.

More nervous than Dawson now, Barry returned to his timings, and the study proceeded as best it could. Across the gangway Saville had somehow assembled part of a cement-mixer inside out, and stood frowning indignantly at his drawing; 'Lias Trigg, marking out, watched the movements of his own plump hand with raised brows of admiration. Around them shears champed, drills shrieked, laden trolleys came and went. Clyde met a gang of platers waiting beside the enormous bare cone of the new weigh hopper: he gave a slow upward movement with his hand, and, obediently, the whole colossal cone gradually rose into the air. Then the platers followed after, while slowly, on slender chains from

13

the overhead crane, gigantic in mid-air, the hopper slid over men and machinery down the length of the shop. It continued to the fitters' section at the far end. There it hovered, and gently settled; then a green mist grew at one corner of it, and crept round it, soon it was half invisible in a green cloud that clung to it and gathered into it: everything there was green, as green as grass. Presently Clyde returned to a large space in the middle of the shop, where already a new hopper was being put together in a hectic iron storm: he waved and called amid a blue blaze of welding that flashed now here now there non-stop, while the broken echoes of sledge-hammering poured from the iron skeleton. The platers reached out through large spaces in the sides to catch curved sheets of steel that hovered towards them. Above the sudden shrill wailing of lathes and drills came the shattering clear crash as a girder came down on the concrete. In a long rumble the overhead crane slid into the rusty haze at the other end of the shop, and returned again, dangling a large incomplete piece of machinery. Underneath it, gently shepherding the iron bulk forward, was the square shape of Foreman Clyde.

4

Ahead of Clyde, hanging from the crane, the cumbersome mass of iron moved smoothly through the air like a complicated armoured satellite: bars and angles of iron, bolts, rivets, rollers, belts, and open ends of tubes and cables, projected from it all round: it was one black tangle of machinery. It stopped over an empty bay, then, in small drops, an inch at a time, it descended, till it scraped on the floor with a low clang like a new bell. Then it settled, so solidly that at once it looked as though it had grown there.

Clyde sighed and relaxed when it touched the ground as if he himself had been holding it up. This machine was the conveyor to go under the new hopper: he still had a large problem with it, but before he could think any more, he had to collect himself. He nodded to the charge-hand, then walked away up the shop, his mind slowly turning as the iron in his pockets quietly stirred and chinked.

At the end of the shop he saw Perce Bowditch, at the profile burner, and went over to him. In the flood of hot sunlight from the open doors, the acid blue flame of the burner was hard to see; the small exhausted face of Bowditch was wrinkled up in the dazzle.

'Perce, are you through with those guard plates yet?'

Bowditch blinked in the sunlight, and looked as though he could burst into tears, 'Oh, Mr Clyde, they're not half done.'

Clyde had known Bowditch decades, he was the slowest plater there: he was so slow that it seemed a miracle. He didn't smoke, chat, doze, or spend half his day in the lavatory, he simply was born slow. The Time Study, in their idiocy, argued that with their system he must work faster, or he'd get no money; but the only upshot was that he got no money. Clyde thought again—it was his dose of tonic every morning—how pointless and cruel the Time Study was.

Bowditch stood scratching the yellow back of his neck, which was criss-crossed with dirty seams; his grey fingers and the light breeze disturbed the lank points of his greasy hair.

'Perce, you've just got to hurry these buggers up.'

A slight starch of dignity stiffened in Bowditch's stoop. 'I go the best road I can, Mr Clyde.'

Clyde shook his head, not angrily, and left. He turned once, to watch Bowditch gradually sliding a sheet of plate under the fizzing blue flame, then walked on, knowing with pleasure that the Time Study, in practice, was useless.

The noise and business of his shop made a kind of peace for him now, in which he could think. He returned to the problem they had with the conveyor. The difficulty was that it shot out too much sand, and yet the sand had to come out at just that speed. The machine needed to work at full-speed, and at half-speed, at the same time: it wasn't possible. Half-a-dozen designers were working on it as though it were the mystery of the earth. Clyde despised them, he knew he would get there first.

Half way down the shop, he stopped and gravely shouted, 'Morning George!' 'Morning Edward!' a grave voice replied. In the deep blue shade of his bay an elderly plater was marking out. George Reynolds was the Time Study's biggest headache: he had been marking out plate so long that he knew everything by heart, and no longer bothered to look at drawings, or even to use rule or measure. Simply, he held up the green job-card at arm's length, then in one movement swung his arm down and across the plate, leaving a firm chalk line that was dead straight all its length. Because he had abandoned all preliminaries his bonus worked out astronomical, and the Time Study had redesigned some of the machinery to keep in check. He got more money than Clyde, but Clyde gazed at him delighted. Then the conveyor came into his mind: his thoughts turned, he knew he was close to the answer, and then he had it.

He hurried back down the shop to the small work-bay which choked on the black iron crag of the conveyor. He started explaining to the charge-hand, Jim Bundy; then he switched on the motor. With a loud clanking the rollers spun, and the thick belt slid round: the flapping and clattering noise filled the bay, but Clyde and Bundy bent down and, reaching close to the cranks and cogs, Clyde explained what he wanted. Bundy could scarcely hear what he said, but he read Clyde's lips and his own mind leapt to meet Clyde's idea. Then he understood, and both men stood up, and laughed out loud as they looked at the conveyor, and visualized it as it would be.

They glanced up at the newly-painted hopper, which towered over them like a hill and glistened grass-green everywhere: the whole of the hopper must stand, the other way up, over the conveyor. Then they returned to the conveyor and although still it clanked and whirled beside them, vibrating and drumming on the concrete, they stood gazing at it like new parents.

*

Clyde walked up his shop, pleased to the centre. As he passed near his office, the door opened, and his clerk Josh, and the works messenger-girl, came out on the balcony: she had just delivered a new batch of time-cards. Clyde gazed at her with pleasure as she pattered down the stairs, and he waited to ask her how his old friend her father, the foreman of the foundry, was keeping; while his large arm of its own will gently squeezed her to him. He was full of goodwill and inquiry: she was marrying one of his platers at the weekend. Then he let her go, and watched after her as she stepped out into the yard, and burst into bright colour. He nodded to Josh, and continued his rounds.

5

A half-strangled electric shriek filled the shop, and the walloping iron din fell away as if stilled by a magician. In the abrupt silence, the singing plater—he did this every day—had timed his last aria so that for the following half-minute, while he switched off the controls of his machine, his voice only climbed and strengthened, note leaping over note from lungs like high-pressure cylinders, till, as he stood unbuckling his satchel, his lower jaw absorbed into his neck, he held the last note unwavering for second on second: then stopped sharply, sat down on a toolbox, and deftly unspun his Thermos cap, conscious but casual among the suspicious, pleased and derisive platers.

All down its length the shop bloomed with sports pages and rustled with greaseproof paper. Barry Spurrier, amazed that he had got through unscathed to tea-break, retreated temporarily to the Time Study office, while Dawson joined Trigg and Saville. 'Lias held out for inspection a plastic mug with a liquid like tar in it which he had just poured out of his Thermos, 'Here, take a squint at that, there's a mug of the old Harry Thickers!'

A driller nearby switched off his machine, and came their way: a short man with a face puckered and pouched all over like a crumpled web with lines of worry, hurt and sceptical humour. He hesitated near them. 'Morning mates!' His bright kindly brown eyes glanced at them nervously; they nodded shortly, and stopped talking till he had passed. The man was a foreigner, a Czech.

They went to the work-bay of a plater called Jenkins, an overflowing lethargic sack of a man who flopped about the shop in loose work-clothes like pyjamas, oil all over, half undone. His face had a sallow, slack fatness; he wore round old-style National Health glasses, and had a skimpy black moustache; he was known in the shop as King Farouk. And he was surrounded by girls. Elsewhere old photos of Monroe and Sabrina quietly aged in odd nooks of machinery; but the canvas-walled work-bay of Farouk was converted, from top to bottom, into a glossy fluttering harem. On white beaches girls the different colours of honey curled towards him, tensing their thighs; big women half-closed their eyes to him in surrender; white-skinned blondes with turned-up noses and nipples were surprised naked in thickets of jungle; girls in overalls unzipped from top to bottom rested impatient tongues between snowy teeth, and coiled and uncoiled, slowly pushing limp hair and cloth back from hot damp skin.

Farouk was involved in Sellotape, placing his latest find, while the platers observed and criticized. In the centre of them was Patrick Collier, who was marrying the messenger-girl at the weekend, and the platers hooted at him for giving up the luscious pleasures of freedom before he'd known them. His bright unlecherous eyes flickered lightly from face to face, while he let on that he was corrupter than all of them. At first they wouldn't have it, but then in mockery they consulted him on the finer points of the pin-ups. 'Hey, Pat, would you call her Michelin X?' 'Well then, young Patrick, I dare say you'd suck raspberry jam off her tits for a thousand year.' Collier laughed, red and glowing as the centre of attention. Saville was not amused; 'Lias Trigg was in his element; the Czech driller, always left out, hovered at the back, showing his teeth in a white wide grin while his eyes were worried.

In the office overhead, Clyde and his clerk sat comfortably at their elevenses. The platers, and the Time Study, imagined that Clyde spent such times contriving ways to harass them, but he was too old a hand to waste his times of rest. He chatted with his clerk.

'Josh, you seen that galvanized that Dan's got up at Assembly?'

Josh's poor eyes blinked and screwed continually behind glasses like the bottoms of bottles, in an ill-shaved face unhealthily swollen, hard and red.

'It's lovely, is it, Mr Clyde?'

'What! It's beautiful. I don't remember when I last saw galvanized like that.'

They mused and chatted quietly about how best Clyde could get some of the beautiful metal round to his house undetected, until, without looking at his watch, Clyde got up. 'Time for the milk round.' As he opened the door, the hooter rose to its long howl. The shop stirred, an axle squealed. There was a sudden crackling, a start of blue glare, and a cement-mixer jumped into silhouette. Engines coughed and revved, the crane ground overhead, and the tap-tap-tap of someone nearby hammering on metal was presently only a delicate pattering, like rain, on the surface of the rising tide of noise that swelled and mounted and dinned through the shop.

The early-morning leisure had disappeared, and the shop was in its main burst of work for the day; Clyde's patrol was a round of troubles he had to deal with at once. The brake press jammed, new plates were missing, a welded flange had come clean off—was the whole order botched? Then, on top of all else, the Time Study came to him, wanting to haggle over the way his men should do their jobs: when he had got rid of the Study, his temper was in shreds. But still he was lugged from one emergency to the next; though however much he did, the list of things waiting to be done only rode away without end. The air of the shop was thick and acid with the sickening mixed smell of coolant, metal and weld; the sun beat on the roof and heated it like a gigantic grill-plate; and the noise, now, was shattering—drills whined, torn metal groaned and shrieked, and everywhere there was hammering. The platers hammered metal round corners to bend it; they hammered it on the floor to get it straight; they worked round the hopper in hammering gangs. The blacksmith brought his sledge-hammer down on the red bar, which his assistant held to the anvil with long spidery claws, in solid crashes so that golden flakes and scales shot off it, in a constant jarring thud that shuddered through the Plate Shop like the beating of its heart. The singing plater still opened his mouth, but now no-one heard his voice. From the loudspeakers a long crackling cry swooped and soared to weird scales of its own: this was the official Music While You Work, though it was lost in the iron music it fed.

The racket went through Clyde's head, and as the crises piled over him he felt worn to his end. Then Bundy sent word that he needed help, if he was to alter the new conveyor in the way Clyde had said. Clyde wanted to send his best plater, Dawson; but then he remembered that Dawson was tied up in a time-study. Hurt and powerless, Clyde cast long eyes at the tiny figure of Dawson with the time-studier, in his buff tunic, beside him; and under the other anxieties his mind

22

ground now in a dry rage on the one slow thought of the constant damage the Time Study did in his shop.

A plater snatched at his elbow. 'Mr Clyde, Mr Clyde, can you come? It's Len Petchey, he's acting up.'

As Clyde hurried to the Drawing Stores, he saw between the jostling men ragged strips of Len Petchey, hunched in his hatch, his brown eyes big as though they had no lids. A muscular plater was fretful and plaintive. 'I've been waiting half hour for one bloody drawing!' Others to similar effect. Clyde picked up the screwed-up knots of drawing-tickets from the counter, and leafed through them. '32769—that's the cowlings, we don't need those till Wednesday. Reg, get started on the drums, will you?' Clyde worked through the tickets, redirecting the platers—it was a point of pride with him to know by the number what each drawing was. He and Petchey ignored each other obviously, till Petchey snapped, 'Chuck that one out, Clyde, blast it! I give it him yesterday.' At Petchey's rudeness, there was a sudden explosion of rage in Clyde: now he was scarcely in control, the appearance of authority was all in all to him. He stamped his anger down, but it pulled into a tight knot at the base of his lungs and hurt there as though his inside caught fire.

As soon as he had finished with Petchey, he made a beeline for Dawson, *still* being time-studied.

*

Down the shop the time-study was now running smoothly. Dawson had got into the rhythm of his work, and Barry Spurrier was under the spell of the exact clean way Dawson's hands lightly lifted the heavy plate, rested it on the bench with a sound quiet as a breath, then brought the metal ruler down on it so exactly that immediately the chalk ran along it in an even line that always met the other lines in a decisive point. It was beautiful work and in the grip of it Dawson was resigned to the fact that he could not go slow; eventually, in a long-drawn-out way, he started chatting to Barry, till it became clear that he was glad to have—what he didn't normally have while working—company.

There was an impatient chink behind Barry, and he turned to find Clyde standing right behind him. He jerked a nod, but there was no flicker of recognition in Clyde's dry, open stare. Barry went on marking times, but was all fumbling and awkwardness now: he also could not stand being watched.

Clyde advanced, and stood making a triangle with Dawson and Barry. And for all the noise in the shop, Barry could only hear now, coming from Clyde, the smothered clanking of muffled bits of iron like the slow turning of old machinery inside him. He kept glancing at the well-known head, which was so much larger than Dawson's or his own: square, red, set into his shoulders so it thrust forward like a creature that never stopped charging its enemy. Clyde must once have had a face like an axe, but time had enlarged and furrowed it: the hard corners of his jaw were dissolved in jowl; his mouth had lost its curving lips and become a rough maw; the skin of his face had pulled in, projecting forward the thickened rubbery cartilages of his nose, and making a long, stubborn upper lip. His eyes gazed out from their overhang like the eyes of an old animal, vigilant, without emotion, giving nothing. He wore an old suit and had the office of foreman, but, as he stood there motionless, large, breathing heavily, what Barry chiefly saw was an old fierce animal, solitary, all purpose worn down to foraging for survival, in a permanent low smouldering anger as age slowly cornered him.

In a rough quiet voice like a file rubbed slowly on wood, Clyde inquired, 'Jim, are you able to get ahead all right?'

Dawson carefully finished drawing his line. 'Can't complain.'

Clyde's profile pointed at Dawson, went jagged with aim, and he started to interrupt: 'Use the scriber.' 'Not that way, man, do it from the left.' 'Is that how you do it?' Each time he interrupted, Dawson stopped to listen, and the time for that operation was lost; and when he prepared to repeat it, Clyde barked, 'For God's sake, don't do it again. Get on, man.' The study now was in ruins. Barry carried on in silence, and Dawson worked as best he could under Clyde's sniping, till suddenly he had had enough, and turned on the foreman. 'For Christ's sake, leave me be, can't you, you're worse than bloody him'—he jerked his head at the time-studier.

Clyde's voice went very quiet. 'Do it your way, Dawson.' He stood watching, while his old dry eyes seemed to recede into his head; for a long time they only heard the slow drag of his breathing, like an old person asleep. But all at once, as if he had just remembered something, he glanced at his watch and said, 'Stop a minute, Dawson. How long have you been on this? Bloody hell, we've more urgent jobs to do than this one. Get over to Bundy and get that conveyor fixed.'

'But I've only got another. . . .' Dawson began, but Clyde cut him short. 'God, man, half the morning's bloody gone, get over there, will you?' Clyde turned sharply, and walked off.

Swearing to himself, Dawson started to leave, without hurry. Barry folded up the wrecked study: this, or something like it, happened every day.

Clyde, however, was only a little way up the shop when he nearly tripped on a laden trolley one of the labourers was dragging towards him. The labourer bawled, 'Mr Cly', Mr Cly"

Clyde stared bemused; for the moment he couldn't connect.

'These for the Pillar Drill, Mr Cly'—who they go to?'

'Oh, what, give them to Pethick.'

Pethick was the foreigner in the shop, the Czech. The labourer exclaimed aghast, 'Pevvick, Mr Cly? These the Offsi' Guars'!'

Clyde, and Barry and Dawson beyond, stared at the stacked plates on the trolley: they were the Time Study's biggest mistake, and had a time that left hours to spare. They were the best job in the shop, and always went to the English driller, Strachey. And Clyde, without thinking, had consigned them to Pethick. The labourer ran on in wonder.

'Eric Strachey won' like this, Mr Clyde. He won' like it at all. No! He won' be pleased!'

Clyde, overwrought already, exploded, 'What the sodded hell do I care about that? Why should Eric Strachey get favours all the time? Let Pethick do them for bloody once — poor bloke, he never gets a go. Take the plates to him.'

Clyde continued glaring as though he were still speaking; he found it gave him pleasure, to do Strachey one in the eye.

The labourer couldn't believe it: that the pecking-line, the great principle of order in the shop, should be violated like this, and by Clyde himself, and on a whim. He turned to Dawson and Barry in staring need of someone to share his moral shock; and Dawson gazed back—there would be hell to pay—but the time-studier, not in that pecking-line, beamed. Then all at once a sudden wild shout went up on the other side of the shop, and all of them ran over there.

6

In the brown shadow under the roof, something moved awkwardly like a creature hanging trapped from a mass of cobweb. As well as the large crane in the centre, the shop had two smaller overhead cranes that ran down the side-aisles, and from one of these a young lad in blue overalls, an apprentice, was hanging by one arm. Somehow the crane had run over his arm and pinned it. The platers had got a ladder up, and one man held the boy under the shoulders to take the weight off his arm, while another leaned out shakily from the same ladder wildly heaving and hurling to push the crane up with his bare hands, though he had no chance of moving it.

The platers milled below, at odds. 'Push to the back!' 'Push to the front, you idiot!' Clyde hit them like a meteor. 'Watts, get crows. Bates, come down off that ladder. Saville, get another bloody ladder.'

'What ladder, Mr Clyde?'

'What ladder? Get Dawkins' bloody ladder.'

Saville ran full pelt down the shop, and stood at the foot of Dawkins' ladder calling, 'Sam, Sam, can I have your ladder, please?' while Dawkins gazed down at him amazed.

'Who went for the nurse?' Clyde shouted; the platers looked at one another. 'Sleath, get over there. And see she gets the ambulance. Oh my Christ, you haven't unloaded the bleeding crane.' He stabbed the push-buttons on the small aluminium control-box dangling under the crane, so the load of piping came down in a clatter. He saw at once what had happened: the apprentice had leaned his ladder against the crane-rail, and had been working up there when the crane came forward and knocked the ladder from under him: as he fell, he grabbed the rail, and the crane went over his arm. It meant that the man working the crane wasn't looking; and it meant that the electrician hadn't turned off the mains before he sent the apprentice to work there. Clyde saw that he himself was not to blame.

'Where is that ladder?' he shouted. Far down the gang-way, they saw Saville flapping and dithering at the bottom of the ladder, while Dawkins, on the top rung, was looking their way, unconvinced, full of misgiving.

'Dawkins!' Clyde roared in a terrible tearing shout that ripped up his throat but carried from one end of the shop to the other. 'Get off that fucking ladder!' As Dawkins looked back then looked at the ground, Clyde howled like bursting thunder, 'Jump you fucking bugger idiot!' Dawkins came down a few rungs, jumped, and he and Saville came running with the ladder.

Clyde looked round, the boy's father had come from the foundry. He did not speak, he was only a white upward face, aghast, mute.

Watts came panting with a sheaf of crowbars. Saville and Dawkins arrived with the ladder, and Dawkins was about to dash up it when Clyde hauled him back, and sent up a big-built plater, Warboys, with a crow; and Surtees, the blacksmith, also with a crow. While they levered in their crowbars, trying to get a purchase, Clyde gazed up at the apprentice. Fortunately he had passed out: in the arms of the plater supporting him, he lightly swayed, his legs and other arm dangling awkwardly; the trapped arm was invisible in a paste of black grease and blood. The agitation round him seemed to go on in slow-motion, making no headway, as if he would hang there for ever.

The electrician had arrived. 'Holmes, do you see? Sending a young lad up there, with the mains left on! Where the hell was your mind?'

'I thought I turned them off.'

Warboys and the blacksmith leaned far back from their ladder, and with all their weight and strength, panting, sweating, shaking, they tugged at the crows. And the crane moved, it trembled up and its front wheels came clear.

'More, more,' shouted the man holding the apprentice.

Warboys and the blacksmith heaved, the crane trembled, the platers gazed upwards fish-mouthed. Clyde turned to a white ripple in the corner of his eye: the works nurse came swinging towards them, clinking her first-aid kit which flashed its red cross. Sleath, who went for the ambulance, jerked and fluttered behind her like a fallen kite. Clyde shouted at her, 'Did you get the ambulance?'

The nurse arrived, lantern-jawed, hefty, brisk on her pins, battered and toughened by decades of factory medicine. 'I'll say if we need an ambulance. You men always cry before . . .'

'Sleath, bloody get up my office, ring for an ambulance this instant. Jenkins get with him, bring the stretcher. Oh you blasted old harridan! Look up there! What! Warboys, stop! Whoa! Hang on! It'll run back!' As he shouted, the tipped-up crane shivered slightly to the right, and Warboys and the blacksmith tried to swing all their weight sideways to steady it. Their ladder shook, and started to slide along the rail.

Several platers grabbed the bottom of it, but their leverage was bad, and while the great bulk of the crane edged to the right, the ladder slipped little inches the other way, so that the two men hung out further and further backwards over space.

'What'll we do? It's going.' Warboys gasped. And there was a further jerk, a sudden movement, and the blacksmith lost his hold. As he slipped, he grabbed the ladder and just hung on. His crowbar came down like a bomb and struck into the concrete with a shattering metal crash. Warboys was left holding all the weight, stretched out over the gulf; and they couldn't free the boy's arm, for his sleeve, half torn off, was wound up with the cogs.

But the crane held; then trembled again; and a faint general whimper came from the platers. They watched the crane as if it had come alive: a huge creature sprawled across the roof.

Warboys was slowly losing. Strain as he did, he hung further out, the crowbar rose, the crane slipped back and down. There was dead silence round, they could hear the shriek of lathes in the Machine Shop across the yard. Then in the centre of the silence, Clyde roared, 'Oh get your finger out, you blasted sodded bone-idle useless bloody pisser, are you so bloody weak and feeble you can't lift the bugger thing half a fucking inch?' He swore himself hoarse in roaring fury, beside himself with contempt, the veins standing out in his red head. And he didn't stop, he shouted on and on. Warboys's face half-showed as he tried to look down, exhausted, helpless, wide with indignation. He couldn't shout back, he lost his temper, his face clenched and went purple and seemed all jaw. He heaved, trembling, and the crane shivered on the crowbar. With bursting face and torn voice Clyde shouted on at Warboys in still rising fury. The insults were an arm with which Clyde himself now reached up and took the weight of the crane and held it where it was. It was beyond Warboys to raise it, but it slipped no further.

A new ladder arrived, and Dawson and Trigg rushed up with crowbars. The platers watched in an awe of horror. Dawson and Trigg took the weight: they leaned back and hung on their crowbars, and the crane rose. A sigh like a breeze passed through the men below.

'Aren't you through with that sleeve yet?' Clyde shouted, but just then the knife went through it, and the boy's arm was free.

'Slowly, carefully !' Clyde called. 'Nurse, tell them what you want.' But while she snapped out her instructions, Clyde also called. 'Steady, steady. That's it. Easy, round. Slowly, slowly.'

The men brought the boy down very slowly, because the ladder was so steep and they needed to support his damaged arm and lower it without shock.

'Easy, easy,' Clyde repeated, his voice lowering in pitch as the boy came down.

The platers pressed close, and with one motion and no bump they received the apprentice in their arms and rested him on the stretcher. His arm was laid in a billowing cloud-cushion of cotton wool that immediately soaked up scarlet. The boy lay back, his plump face white, his short pointed nose jutting up pert; he must be unconscious, but his eyes were half-open, looking up to the roof of the shop. The nurse was absorbed and efficient, tending the arm; the boy's father stooped beside her, in the way, at a loss. Then, following after, she bossed the two men with the stretcher to the doorway, to wait for the ambulance.

Warboys, who was fat and florid as well as strong, sat

back against a bench, almost passed out, drenched and sodden with sweat. The platers realized how quiet the shop was, and they all started to talk.

The ambulance was an age; eventually there was a clamour of bells outside. Through the tunnel under Clyde's office, there was a sudden scurry and a glitter of chrome as the stretcher was lifted in, then the ambulance drove away, bells shrilling.

The platers slowly collected their ladders and crowbars, and dispersed. First near at hand, then at the far end, machines coughed and started.

The father went in the ambulance, but now the other relatives had arrived: a sister from the typing pool; a cousin, in a white shirt, from the Drawing Office; an uncle, in a suit, in square rimless glasses, from Invoices. The uncle was beside himself with anger and battered the sister with legal advice, while tears streamed down her face; the cousin looked on blankly, an empty, young, blank face.

Clyde; and Forbes, the Production Controller; and the electrician; and Strudwick, the Works Manager; and the man who was working the crane, all stood in a huddle, talking busily. Every few seconds the voice of the electrician rose, 'I turned it off. I'm sure I turned it off.'

7

In the canteen, the platers sat with the platers, the machinists with machinists, the fitters (cream of the cream) with the fitters. Mrs Logie ladled out the sodden cabbage in wet wallops on to thick grey plates that looked to be made of concrete: the atmosphere was clammy with the steam of greens and gravy. Stone-deaf Billy Bailey, a figure of fun, looked round bewildered, bawled at by impeded men with trays; while guidance was given and way made for the two blind telephonists to a sheltered corner table, where they ate sensitively and chatted chirpily with raised heads, like two birds. A welder rushed up to his mates with excited eyes. 'Hey, Jack! Did you see his arm, then? It was hanging off at the shoulder. Hanging off, it was!' The father and sister of the injured boy weren't there, but the cousin and uncle sat in the middle of the room, accepting advice and giving their views with a shine of importance. Stuck with the other disreputables, Trout the labourer hooted at the thought of the dire ructions there would be when Strachey found out the best job in the works had gone to Pethick. King Farouk wiped his plate with his bread until it was spotless, then slowly sat back and closed his eyes. Behind the counter the harassed kitchen-girls relaxed and finally sat to eat.

After lunch the sun was scorching, and the glare on the newly-painted machines was so dazzling that it hurt to look at them; mostly the men lounged under the large canopies for the lorries. Ragged tears in the corrugated iron sprinkled spots of sunlight among the shadowy lean of men, picking out the peak of a cap, an oily nose, a brown, drowsed comfortable face.

The typists loitered down the dusty cul-de-sac beside the works, and climbed over the railway-line to the abandoned sand-pit beyond. They sat down beside the artificial lake filling the largest pit, in the shadow of an old crane that had lost its works, and was just one gaunt rust-crusted skeleton crowning the squat sandhill: its chains rattled and clinked occasionally. The lake was a round still expanse of blue-white light, the willows and sedges grown up around it stirred quietly with a sound no louder than cloth moving on cloth. The typists sat round Fern, the messenger-girl, rediscussing the arrangements for her wedding at the weekend: she insisted she would wear a white trouser-suit. 'You're never.' 'I am.' They were tickled in their scepticism; except for Strudwick's secretary, a pale exhausted girl who sat apart throwing cake-crumbs to the tiny black fish that darted through the shadows: she moaned out loud, 'I'm on the shelf.' The others rallied round, making a low ripple of chatter as they lay on their backs in the shade, half-watching the pairs of turquoise-blue damsel-flies that flicked among the reeds.

The driest of the platers went to the main gate, and squatted on the low brick wall that penned a narrow queue of geraniums along the frontage of the factory. They sat in a line, studying the heavy traffic and smoking, and this line leaned progressively further forward to either end, like a bent fan, to hear what was said in the middle. In the middle was

'Lias Trigg, and next to him. a plater who sat with a large cardboard box between his legs: every few months he brought along his latest handiwork to show the others.

'What you got in that box, then, Ben?'

'He's got his balls in there, ain't you?'

'Keeps them on ice, does he?'

'Christ almighty, have you seen the size of them?'

'Lias Trigg gave the box a gentle kick. 'Put them on the counter, Ben. Let's have a butcher's.'

Ben got up, and lifted the box onto the wall. He had had polio, and as he turned his gammy leg flung out to one side, and came down with a painful jolt. With ceremony and tenderness he unfolded the flaps of the box, and parted the newspaper wrappings inside. Then he lifted out, like eggs from a nest, two footballs, brand new. One was clear white, one was bright orange; they were spotless and gleaming.

The balls were passed out gingerly, with tips of fingers, to either end of the line, 'United use them balls, don't they, mate?' 'Yeah, and City too.' Ben explained again how it was, when he had done everything else from the inside, that he stitched in the last panel. The platers enjoyed the firm clean brightness of the new leather, and the strong brown stitching that held the panels together. They looked wistfully at Ben, who was a teenage star player before the polio.

Nutty Saville had a doubt. 'They're good, Ben, but I'd say they're a sight easier to make than rugger balls.'

'No, Nutty. Rugger balls are easier.'

'Well, I wouldn't have thought that, Ben. Rugger balls are a harder shape.'

'Ah, but there's fewer pieces, Nutty, and they're easier to sew.'

'Easier to sew?' Saville hooted, but since he was obviously

in the wrong the others piled on him to shut him up. '*Course*
they are!' 'You *are* an arse, Nutty.'

The orange football reached King Farouk at the end of the
line; he turned it slowly in his hands, admiring, then said
loudly, 'Ah, Ben, you won't want for work.'

All down the line, the platers' faces dropped. 'How's that?'
they asked unnecessarily. 'Lias Trigg jumped in. 'We won't
want for work, not with the talents we've got here. There's
Billy Wilmot, he can sing for his supper. There's Trout, old
labourer, he can piss higher and gob further than is known to
be humanly possible. And there's me—I can paint!'

The platers leaned in, at this revelation that 'Lias Trigg
was a covert artist. 'Lias seated himself more comfortably. 'It
was after the war, I was a 'prentice then, and they put us to
paint the silo wall. There was an old boy lived there, where
the tool works is now, old boy called Carruthers, had a small-
holding, kept a pig. Well, it was a quiet day, and you know
we got to pissing about with that paint a bit, and that old boy,
he was out there stitching the holes in his chicken-wire at the
time, and he called out something to me, that gave me —
offence. So when he went down the market, I set to work.'

'I bet that was a picture and a half.'

'I didn't paint no picture, Jim.'

'Lias paused, serious, and Victor Watts continued. "Lias
is an arse. He come back to his bench in the shop, and he was
all— all *demure*. I never seen him like it. Half hour later, old
Carruthers come in. He was hopping mad: he was red in the
face: he was shouting. He come in the shop, and he had that
pig on a length of string, and do you know that pig had yellow
stripes and blue spots all over it. He brought that old pig right
down the bloody Plate Shop to Clyde's office. Did Clyde hit
the roof? He went through it!'

The platers laughed, and loudest of all came the satisfied, remembering laugh of 'Lias.

King Farouk was patient. He waited till the end, he laughed a bit, and then he reverted. 'Ah well, 'Lias, seeing you're a *Picasso*, then, I dare say you won't want for work, not like some of us'—he looked round severely—'not if we all get flogged off.'

The platers cursed him. 'You cheerful bugger—if you know so fucking much, why don't you come along to the union meeting this evening and put us in the picture?'

'What! There's Mike and Bernie Winters on the telly —I don't give them a miss!' Now he had depressed the others, Farouk was cheerful.

A plater said, 'We should take the place over, run it ourselves.'

'That'd be bloody good.'

The platers laughed at the idea with pleasure, till Saville said, indignant-perplexed. 'Well! I don't know about that! I mean—who'd be Foreman?' Then they laughed at him.

'Who will be Foreman?' 'Lias asked.

There was a pause; the platers gradually woke to the fact that Trigg was speaking seriously.

'How's that, 'Lias?' 'What are you on about?' they asked.

'Well, how long do you give Clyde?'

'Dunno, he's been here bloody ages, hasn't he? I reckon he was standing in the middle of a field here, when they come along and built the place.'

'So what? The way he carries on, I'd give him a month. I'd give him days.'

The platers were dubious. The idea that Clyde might be replaced had hovered on the breeze for weeks, and there was no smoke without fire. But Clyde was rooted so deep they could hardly believe it. None the less, the idea stuck, and in spite of what they had just been saying with Farouk, they presently fell to discussing the succession.

Watts asked, 'Who do you back for Foreman, then. 'Lias?'

'I know who it ought to be.'

'What, Dawson?'

'Of course Dawson. Who's better than him?'

'Ah no well yes, he's a good plater, Dawson. I said, he's a good plater, Dawson.'

Nods rippled back and forth along the line.

'What would Clyde do?'

'He could set up in a blessed scrap iron shop, couldn't he? He could flog off what he's got in his pockets, for a start, that'd keep him going for a year and a half!'

'Yeah, phew ! He wouldn't half go up the wall.'

'Go up the wall? No, Vic, he'd go mad. He thinks he is the place, he thinks it's all him.'

'It'd be hard for Clyde. Not like Ben.'

'Ah, Ben won't want for work.'

They had come to a pause, and sat in thought while their hands still shunted the two new footballs down the line, turning them slowly in tender admiration.

The plater at the end of the line was looking in to the centre; then his face tautened. His eye was caught by something coming down the road towards the factory. Then one by one, down the line, all the platers turned their heads, and stared, and their faces quietened into one expression, as though this expression lay underneath all the others, a low blank dazzle of surprise and pain. Yet all they saw was a large caravan towed by a Land-Rover. The Land-Rover was spotless and shining, painted all over as white as sugar or snow. The caravan was huge, and featureless, with nothing on it to say what it was; it was made of an odd glassy alloy.

The Land-Rover and caravan slowed as they came to the works gate, and drove in. The platers got off the wall, disturbed, and started to follow. As they walked down the driveway, the Land-Rover passed them again, driving off.

They found the caravan parked in the courtyard between the Plate Shop, the Machine Shop and the Foundry. It was locked up. The odd metal it was made of, with its dulled shine, was filled with faint reflections, drained of colour, of everything round it. Any steadying props it had were out of sight, and it rested above the ground as though it had no weight. It gleamed lightly, silverily, like something made of mercury.

The platers coming in for the afternoon shift stopped by the caravan, and stood looking at it, talking quietly. There was a noise of bikes and cars beyond, more and more men poured into the yard, and paused there, till the caravan stood in the centre of a crowd. Platers craned on tip-toe, trying to see inside, but the windows were greenly black like the windows of an ambulance. There was no light inside.

Presently there was a further disturbance: Foreman Clyde walked into the yard, and the platers deferred and made way for him. He stopped by the caravan, and a pucker slid down his face like the shadow of a hand.

'Is Crowley here?' he asked the men near him.

The inquiry went round; but Crowley had not come yet, there was only the caravan.

The caravan was still and locked and gave nothing away; eventually, subdued, uncertain, the men drew off from it, and slowly went into the workshops, murmuring, 'Has anyone seen Crowley?' 'When is he going to come?'

8

In the sweltering afternoon, when the dazzling summer sun turned the Plate Shop into a kiln, and no one could work with a will, Warboys strolled over to Strachey at the Pillar Drill. He called out, 'Seen the wheel-house, then ?' but he got only a quick flash of a narrow vinegar face, and Strachey turned his back on him.

'Here, Eric, what's up the spout?'

Strachey drove the bit of his drill hard into the shrieking metal, the milky coolant spoked out in a wet explosion, and the fine slivers of silver metal, uncoiling round the bit, writhed as though he were boring Medusa's head.

'Tell us, Eric.'

Strachey turned. 'Blimey O'Riley, Nosy Parker's not in it! What do you wanna know for, eh?' But he switched off the drill, and presently volunteered, 'You know them Off-sides?'

'The jammy ones? Got another load of them, have you? You're in clover there, boy!' Warboys shouted, then stopped dead.

'*He*'s given them to Pethick.'

'He can't do that ! You always do them plates.'

Strachey swore, as he unstuck a fag-end and with it a sliver of lip. 'Oh, I know why it is. I told him to his face, I don't mind the Time Study. I don't work better than I did, but I get a bloody sight more cash. I said that this morning. He didn't like it. That's why I said it.'

Warboys shook his head in slow heavy swings as though he had a cannon-ball inside it. These jobs were Strachey's, everyone knew that. A hot itching flush crept upwards from his neck, and when he had a good head of steam, he burst out, 'Bloody little foreigners, they think they run the show!'

A long shrug wove down Strachey's emaciation. Warboys looked full at him in indignant commiseration: he was a chargehand, he felt the strength in him that had lifted the crane, and he took the responsibility. 'Don't you fret, matey. We'll soon put this to rights!' He shouted 'Trout!' at the top of his voice, and the stooping labourer who brought the plates, with his blackened depressed face and awkwardly long arms, came over to them at his convenience, dragging an empty trolley.

'Trout, you come with me,' Warboys said, and looked at Strachey cheerily for thanks. Strachey replied with an uncomfortable fidget. Warboys saw that was all he'd get.

'Fucking foreigners!' he muttered, and set off up the shop.

They made a small procession, Warboys big with rage and duty, holding his pace back to a solemn stalk so as not to lose Trout; Trout bent and tugging; and the unoiled trolley jerking and squeaking in the rear. As they went, Warboys stoked his anger, for it was only when he was beside himself with indignation that he felt sure and strong. Then he reckoned he had the Character which he envied in Strachey, and which made him Strachey's admirer and doormat. At the end of the gangway, he saw Pethick in his bright red and blue shirt, raising and lowering the handle of the drill.

When he arrived, Pethick glanced at him with his kindly brown eyes. It was this look in his eyes that helped the platers decide he was weak and had a screw loose: it infuriated Warboys.

'Yes?'

'I've come for the plates.'

There was a slight pause while Pethick made sure he had heard right: his English had reached a certain point and then stopped. He pointed to the stack of blue-grey metal sheets, with the rows of chalked rings on them where the drill-holes were to go.

'The Offside Guards, you mean? I have not done those yet.'

'No, and you ain't gona neither, matey! Old Eric Strachey's after them.'

The net of lines on Pethick's face slowly pulled tight. 'Clyde gave these plates to me.'

'Dammit, Pethick, you blasted well know those plates are Strachey's. He always does them. You know that.'

'Clyde gave them to me,' Pethick repeated, but less

certainly, for the outrage in Warboys's speech was telling.

Warboys was too furious to say another word. He picked up one of the plates, and holding it against his stomach like a tea-tray he bawled at Pethick, 'I don't know what you're complaining about. You never had'em before.'

Pethick always had accepted the pecking-order with a quietness that to most of the platers made him seem mental, though for him it was the way to keep sane. He did protest now—but what he said was lost in the crash, as Warboys banged the plate down on the trolley.

'Here, Trout,' he said roughly, 'give us a hand.' They stacked the plates on the trolley while Pethick watched them with a shake in his hard breathing. When all the plates were loaded, Warboys himself took the trolley handle—and Pethick stepped in front of him, barring his way.

'No, Warboys,' he said, not loudly, but with a violent push of air from his lungs. 'Why you take—my job? Who says you do this? You think—what you think? Who—' He broke off, he was so moved, his English broke down. He stood before Warboys, furious and helpless, so Warboys saw he had only to hold his ground.

'Do you mind?' he said, after a pause, truculent, and he jerked Pethick aside with his head. Wondering at himself, Pethick stepped aside.

Warboys set off, but presently gave the trolley-handle to Trout. Trout had not oiled his trolley-wheels in a year, and it was slave-labour to pull it loaded.

Pethick watched the procession move back up the shop: the loaded labouring trolley scraping and squealing, the lean toiling hump of Trout, bent double, and the shoulders-back bulk of Warboys beyond. Pethick started after them, but when he had only gone a little way he stopped and turned

43

back. His face had gone tight and dry.

Strachey, at the other end of the gangway, was absorbed in rolling a cigarette.

Warboys cried warmly, 'Here's yer plates, matey!'

Strachey frowned.

Warboys's face fell, it tumbled. 'Don't seem too glad to have'em,' he grunted. 'I had the devil's own business getting them. Little bleeding foreigners, they think they own the place!'

There was an uncomfortable sidle in Strachey's lean on the drill. Contemptuously he brought out, 'Let the little bugger have'em.' His face involuntarily screwed in a grimace. Now honour was satisfied, he reckoned to be generous, but it hurt.

All Warboys's stoutness worked explosively. Strachey hitched his weight from one shoulder to the other, and called out. 'Ta for your trouble, mate. It was good of you.'

'Good on me!' Warboys swore till he ran out, and ended up plaintive, 'Are you going to take these plates, or aren't you?'

Strachey considered. 'Nah, nah, take'em back.'

'What! Have I got to take'em back? Sod and bugger that!'

Strachey lowered his head in an apologetic hunch that was also a shrug. His sharp tongue darted across the end of his cigarette, and he carefully planted it on his lip. Warboys looked round like a frightened horse. 'Trout!' he roared, 'You take these plates back up Pethick's, and tell him he can do them after all!' Labourers were at the bottom of the pecking-line, even Pethick could have bossed Trout.

Trout glimmered at Warboys through glazed eyes, and croaked. 'Tell'im yerself.'

Warboys flung round and stamped back up the shop. So the procession returned again: Warboys black with dudgeon,

Trout cursing his trolley, and the trolley now grinding loudly, and issuing a piercing wail. The other platers came to the gangway, tickled.

'Coals to Newcastle, eh?' 'Here, Stirling, don't take the corners too hard.'

Warboys proceeded, solid with contained rage. But it was a good walk to Pethick's bench, especially long-drawn-out with the trolley so decrepit. Warboys chivvied Trout, to no effect. The journey took an age, and Warboys' fury wore thin. The heat overwhelmed him. He saw Pethick watching him come, with a fixed stare, and he took umbrage: it was a rude stare. But it told, and Warboys came up to Pethick hunched and sheepish. Then, just as he arrived, the front axle of Trout's trolley finally wore through, the trolley went down on one knee, and with a shattering clatter and crash the plates came spilling across each other over the concrete floor like a deck of cards. If anyone were in the way, he'd have his foot cut off. Warboys felt utterly made a fool of. He slunk up to Pethick, and asked in a soft, doughy, dingy sort of voice:

'Er—Pethky—did you want your plates back?'

'So, Warboys, these plates are not up to snuff? I wish you tell me earlier, I get better ones.'

Warboys fidgeted, and nervously wheedled, 'These are very good plates, Pethky. They've got a very good time on them.'

'Is not the time I care about. I care about the way I am dealt with here. You take my work away, you bring it back. Don't do it, do do it. You think you are foreman, or something?'

Pethick had come close to Warboys, whose plump hands fluttered weakly like drugged doves. Warboys shouted out, shrill, 'You'd better do them plates, Pethky!'

'Oh, I got to do them, do I?'

'Yes, you'd better fucking do them, Pethick, you better bloody had!' Warboys was more in his element shouting, and prepared to let go at full pitch. But just then a dinning engine nearby was switched off, the operator wanted to hear the row. In the sudden quiet Warboys's voice sounded loud in his ears: he lost his nerve again and faded out.

Pethick said quietly, 'Don't shout at me, Warboys. I have enough of being shouted at. As to the plates, I am not interested now. You can pick them up, and take them back to Strachey.'

'I shan't bloody touch those buggers again!'

Pethick returned to his bench and unfolded the drawing for another job.

'I'll go and see Clyde!' Warboys shouted, his voice singing high.

'Go and see him.'

'Is that what you want?' He hung and dithered.

Pethick looked critically at the drawing.

'Right then!' Warboys shouted. He turned and went. A watching plater called, 'Leave it, Wobbles! Let things cool off!' But Warboys did not stop, he was working up in offended virtue. He strode away, the thick gristle and brawn of his neck showing scarlet.

9

Clyde, at this time of the day, looked more like a lorry-driver in the midst of repairs, than the picture of Authority. His jacket would be hanging, ominous and unapproached, on some hook or lever in a remote corner of the Plate Shop, and he walked over to Pethick a harassed middle-aged man with his sleeves rolled up and his white forearms marbled with oil. His face, which in the close dusty heat of the shop looked as if it were made of red cork, was streaked and stained with black where he had rubbed it in perplexity. His trouser pockets bulged with the thick corners of spanners, and he moved in his own light, clanking music. He did not look like a man to move awe in anyone, but the platers gathering round Pethick moved back in a wave as he arrived, and his deep voice, hoarse from shouting, reproachful, worn-out beyond exhaustion, asked, 'What is this, Mares?'

'I am glad you come, Mr Clyde. I tell—'

'Warboys told me what happened, Mares. But you've got the plates back now—will you do them or not?'

Ordinarily, Clyde's tone with Pethick was compassionate-avuncular, as though Pethick, being foreign, could not be completely a man. But now, behind this tone, was a low seething impatience, as if he could only, just, with difficulty, hold back the tiger.

Pethick expected to do the plates in the end, but couldn't think of this till he had had the Warboys business out. 'Warboys told you? You listen to Warboys? What did Warboys say?'

'Leave it, Mares. Drop it. I don't want to hear your side. You've got the plates. Will you do them?'

'Don't tell me to do them like that, Mr Clyde.'

'Dammit, man, do you want me to ask you on bended knees?'

'Don't make pantomime, Mr Clyde, you listen—'

But Clyde no longer could listen. In the slow urgent voice he would use to a child who had exasperated him beyond measure, he explained, 'You've got the plates back now, Mares. I gave them to you specially. Is this the thanks I get?'

Pethick heard the tone, not the words, and suddenly all the English he needed came to him, and he said in a louder voice than the platers had heard him use before:

'Mr Clyde, I will tell you my side. I was just going to do these guards when Warboys came. He took them—'

'Don't tell me all the ins and outs,' Clyde began, when, to his frank astonishment, to the watching platers' helpless wonder, Pethick loudly spoke over him. 'I said, he should not take them. But he just took them. It was very rude! For years and years I put up with it. I do nothing, I think, well, I am foreign, is a serious thing. But this, from Warboys, is the straw on the camel, now I say, No, I will not be pushed.'

Pethick stopped, surprised himself: something cooped up had stretched itself easily. At the weird reversal in Pethick, a needle feeling like jealousy pierced Clyde. He brushed away Pethick's speeches with a jerky thrust of his wrist that clipped Pethick's hand, and shouted with a tremor, 'I won't stand here talking to you. I've a hundred and one bleeding things to do. I'll leave you to it now, and I'll be back in ten minutes. If you've not started on those plates by then—if you haven't—you'd better have, that's all.' He marched off through the shop in a jangle of iron.

Round Pethick the unsettled platers blew this way and that. 'Hey, old Pethky, you told him, eh?' 'This'll come to a bad end, I can feel it coming on.' But there was a new friendly tone towards him: Victor Watts smiled at him as one manly man to another and said, 'Phew! We stand up for our rights in this shop!'

Pethick was in a trance. He shook his head, to shake the noise and heat out of it. Eventually he started towards the plates, but after what had happened, he couldn't just give in. He stood locked, while the platers battered him with contradictory advice.

Before the ten minutes were up, Clyde came tramping back. He found Pethick in front of his drill, with his arms tightly folded: he was as stiff as a wooden figure, his eyes did not move in his head.

'Well, Mares?'

Pethick only stood rigid, and stared: evidently he could not speak.

'Pethick, have you started on those plates?'

Pethick opened his mouth, and from it came a faint click like a dry straw snapped. He shook his head with a jerk.

'Will you do them?'

Pethick shook all over, and suddenly roared in Clyde's face at the top of his voice, 'No!'

A barrier broke, everything got simple. 'That's it. Get your cards. You're out.' Clyde walked briskly off, he had more important concerns.

Pethick's audience thinned.

'What did he mean?' Pethick asked.

'Yer aht, mate,' a stolid voice said.

Pethick blinked; a heavily built plater said hoarsely, ''Sright, mate . . . 'stough . . . 'slife.'

10

Wally Reed, the man in the shop who came nearest to being Pethick's friend, slipped back and forth in front of him, muttering about the union meeting, but Pethick could not connect with what he said. He was dimly aware that while the near platers were shearing off, those further away were strolling over to look at the sacked man.

George Reynolds, the elderly plater who was beyond rule and measure, took a roundabout route through the shop that brought him, presently, to Clyde's office. He had been Shop Steward many years, and though the shop wasn't his any more, he had a responsibility.

He climbed the iron staircase and opened the door of the high office. Clyde glanced up briefly, caught. He muttered 'Oh, George,' and returned to his cards. He was surrounded with the stiff buff and green job-cards which the messenger-girl had brought from the Time Study. They stood on his bench in wads and stacks, or were fanned out or just thrown across each other, and he was trying to sort them. But he kept interrupting himself, he didn't care if he mangled the cards, and the confusion only got worse.

Reynolds deliberately sat and spread himself, and for all Clyde's fret he was happy to sit there waiting. Though the office looked like a prison-turret from the shop-floor, inside it was a fresh oasis from the shop's heat and racket. Clyde had the window onto the roof open, and a breeze came in with the bright sun. Everything in the cluttered eyrie was familiar to Reynolds: the two swivel-chairs which Clyde and his clerk had half bust, half worn to their shape, over the years, with their faded leaky cushions; and the innumerable makeshift little drawers and shelves that were nailed to the wall, or piled on the bench or slung under it. On the bench the drawings and job-cards leaned against any support in high shaky towers, and everywhere among them, humping up or poking out, and now constantly clattering to the floor as Clyde brushed darkly past, were the tools and wrenches and screw-gauges that Clyde could not find room for in his suit. All the cards and papers there were faded by the strong sunlight that searched out every inch of the office, and lay in a faint patchwork of half-bleached yellows and greens.

At last Clyde stopped, stared fiercely at the twisted cards clenched in his horny hand, then, just as he did when he had a good hand at brag, he muttered at them, 'Get out!' and chucked them across the bench. He dumped himself in his chair. 'What do you want, George?'

'Edward, ain't you got more paperwork here than you can properly handle?'

Clyde's eyes widened at the liberty—and Reynolds went on, 'Isn't it Josh's job to do the paperwork?'

'What the blazes are you on about, George? Josh doesn't know what's what with the bleeding Time Study no more than I do. And he can't hardly see to read these blasted cards!' He flared with accusation, as though Reynolds were responsible for Josh's bad eyes.

'Wouldn't it be an idea to get a clerk who could see?'

'Oh yes? And what would become of Josh? By Christ, George, I never thought I'd hear that from you. Thirty year he's been with me. And he'd be out on his ear, he'd be in the gutter!'

'Oh, do you mean like Pethick?'

Clyde momentarily sparkled as he found out the old Shop Steward in Reynolds; but his face quickly went beset and peevish. 'You know I hate to sack a man. It turns me over. But there, it's done now.'

But Reynolds would not let it lie. His keen sunk eyes, with their wide lids cupped round them, rested lightly on Clyde as he expanded on the understandableness of Clyde's spur-of-the-moment decision, which Clyde was a large enough man to take back. Clyde's chair began cumbersomely to fidget and creak. He kept turning to the waiting cards, and when Reynolds bore down on the question, should Pethick be taken back, Clyde snapped, 'Cut it short, George. I've so bloody much on hand, I can't spend all day talking about Pethick. Do you know how much I've got to cope with here? Do you have any idea?'

Reynolds blinked: his plan was that as Clyde got fed up with the harangue, he would say, 'So, George, you think I should take him back?' He would say, Yes, Clyde would do nothing, and they would talk some more: this would happen twice, and then when Clyde said a third time, 'So, George, you reckon I should take him back?' Reynolds would say nothing, Clyde would take him back, and that would be the end of it. But it had not gone that way today, and Reynolds saw that he had no chance. None the less he said in answer to Clyde's 'Do you have any idea?'—

'A good amount, Edward, but it's Pethick's—'

'A good amount? Do you see these cards? That's yesterday. That's last week. That's last month. It's more than I can handle.' He was out of his chair now, waving handfuls of cards in Reynolds's face. 'I ask you, George, what am I? I used to be something called a Foreman in this shop. I didn't need cards. I had it all up here, what *cards* they sent, I bunged in the bin. But I knew where every drill-hole was, and every bleeding rivet. But now, with this *Time and Motion*, you ask me how it is. I'll tell you. They've got every blessed job chopped up so fine *their* way that every blasted blighted piddling little wiggle of a screw has got a ticket tied round its neck, and all I bloody do, is, I run round and dish out the tickets! Foreman I'm not Foreman here any more. I'm not hardly the office-boy. I'm the bleeding skivvy!'

Reynolds saw he must head Clyde off, but Clyde was too quick for him. 'And if the men don't know how to do something, do they come and ask me? Oh no, no hope of that. Straight round the bleeding Time and Motion, that's where they go, knacking and jawing on in there for hours on bloody end. They used to think a job was a job, now it's all in bits and pieces, and each bit is a minute, and time's money you know, and I know you can't make a truck-mixer come out like a Savile Row suit, but by Christ I see some mucky jobs leave my shop these days. Oh, look at the little lambs!' He rubbed furiously with his fist on the dirty window, and peered through. 'There's Trigg and Saville, nothing better to do than stand there gabbing. And Wilmot in those damned dungarees, what's he doing? Singing! What the fuck has he got to sing about? They don't know what responsibility is. And they get more take-home pay than I do, half of them—you do, don't you? And, what, Trigg and Saville still jabbering. Oh by Christ!' He stumped out onto the stair-head; Trigg and Saville jumped out of their skins at the stridor from on high. Clyde roared them back to work, then came slamming back into his office inflamed, out of breath, yet shouting as though he were still outside. 'And the tickets! Take this ticket for the chassis frame that I'm looking for now. Is it here? Here? Oh where the bleeding hell is the blasted sodded puking bugger?' He banged on the desk, and the paper towers rocked and tottered.

He stopped himself, and stood heavily getting his breath back, gazing at his desk. Presently he started to pick at the cards, then said, 'I don't know what you're waiting for, George. I've nothing to say about Pethick.' Then, more querulously, 'I tried to help him out, it wasn't good enough for him. So he can clear out. I gave him rope, he hung himself, and you can sit there pulling long faces if you like.' At last he faced Reynolds, working up to full anger. 'But I bloody well wonder, Reynolds, what business you think it is of yours. You reckon you can come in here, tell me to my face—God, man, do you see what the time is? I reckon you'd better get back to your bench.'

Reynolds got up with difficulty and slowly walked out of the office.

At the moment the door shut, Clyde started, and glared wildly and gasped as though Reynolds had taken with him all the air in the room. He came to, and wandered in his office, murmuring, 'What possessed the man?'

The door opened slowly, and his clerk Josh came in. Blinking continuously behind his thick glasses, he asked, 'Was that George Reynolds, Mr Clyde?'

'Yes! Bloody fool ! What did he want to come and raise Cain about Pethick for? I thought he had more sense.'

Josh wrinkled his eyes as though they hurt. 'What is this with Pethick, Mr Clyde? I just seen him and Reed talking nineteen to the dozen to the Shop Steward, Hawkins. You know they've got a meeting today. You don't want trouble with union now, Mr Clyde, really.'

Clyde would say nothing to that. Josh's shiny red forehead corrugated, but without further inquiry he sat down and reached for the cards. Clyde also sat, utterly jaded. The exhausted sour displeasure he was in now, was more than he knew what to do with. He had to go carefully, any trouble he made could get out of hand and finish him, but all he could do was sit there, gazing out through the window, stopped dead.

The view he saw was the view he must by now have spent years of his life looking at. It stretched on and on for ever, in zig-zag ups and downs, in the brown late afternoon: scarps, cliffs and peaks of the neglected roofscape of corrugated iron—crusted with bird-droppings, stained, freckled and scabbed with rust, holed with jagged gaps where the iron had rotted through and crumbled up in brittle flakes. Hard-edged against the sky, the blunt hoods of the blast-furnaces tipped towards each other like old women conspiring. The derrick there was working, presently a wheelbarrow piled with scrap was hoisted into sight. It swung and bounced crazily in mid-air, and up-ended itself into the furnace-top: a gust of fire and smoke struck out, and the barrow rocked down again below the roofs. Nearer at hand thin white pipes spidered up and squirted sudden tight scalding jets of steam; and at intervals through the roofing grew the main chimneys, tall, even aluminium stems, with steps spiralling round them going nowhere. They were matt and velvety at the top, as if with caked soot. From them, in sudden gushes, turbid black smoke burst upwards, tore apart slowly, and dragged across the sky.

Josh, sitting next to Clyde, spread the cards on the bench, and, cocking his head, screwing up his eyes, holding the cards to the light, he gradually arranged them in separate orderly stacks.

11

When Clyde was first made Foreman, the firm made cement-mixers only: the spindly 5NT for boys and Sunday builders; the four-wheeled 7NT with its large globe like a bomb; and the 10NT where the huge drum, in its square shell of armour-plating, ground slowly like a mill-stone set in a tank. Later the firm expanded and took in truck-mixers, plaster-mixers, drills and plant—iron funnels bigger than houses that paid out in a trickling thread a crushing tonnage of cement. It came to engross every machine that had to do with building, and its machines were to be found swallowing and churning and pouring out in France and Spain, in Arabia and India, in Australia and Latin America: everywhere they stirred the glue that held the modern world together. Towers stalking deserts of cityscape; great vats with slim waists holding hot lakes that steamed slowly; huge mushroom-shaped bowls that held a flood in mid-air as in a huge hand, cupping upwards, on a slender wrist; cliff-walls of dam propping a deluge: the cement that held all of them whole, that was nine-tenths of their bulk, was compounded, stirred and brought to life in the churning iron wombs the factory multiplied. And the metal they were made from was all of it chalked out, cut and burned out, was riveted, welded and banged together, in the vaulted two-acre hangar of the Plate Shop: and of the Plate Shop, barely into his thirties, Clyde was made Foreman.

It brought out powers in Clyde he did not know he had. He took to heart the responsibility for the whole shop, and the fine tree of his nerves came live as with electric current. He half-knew by instinct, and quickly knew thoroughly, how all the machines there worked: he had always been fascinated by the delicate cogs and gears and the fine maze of wiring that controlled the cumbersome iron, and now all their mass rested easily on his shoulders. When one broke down, he stripped it there and then himself, and what he didn't know, his quick grasp guessed. He would carpet the floor with an engine in a gleaming mazy litter of gears and sprockets and junctions over which the operator scratched his head and chewed his lip, in mingled misgiving, awe and dry speculation about the day Clyde would get it wrong. But Clyde darted among the bits, filed a tooth and welded a flange, and in a twinkling the scattered paraphernalia danced back into its casing and worked like silk or music. His power was based in this, he had no pomp, he spent the day in and out of machinery, his sleeves rolled up, smeared and dripping with oil. He had a sufficient way with the men, but they were chiefly struck by his admiration for machinery that worked exactly and well, and by his simple disgust at a ragged cut left by the shears, a drill-hole on the skew, a bend out of true. So involved, he began to invent, he pursued ideas that simplified, which no-one else had. The platers saw his mark on each machine that went through.

But inventions that made the firm thousands of pounds brought Clyde no special bonus; and though his interest flowed from day to day, perhaps it all flowed nowhere, for every machine they made would one day be so much rusty scrap. His job was thankless, battered by both sides. In the early days there had been fights, men hit each other with hunks of iron and one man had his back broken. Clyde's only way of stopping these was to become more deadly with a crowbar than the platers: thereafter, he maintained a clear pecking order so everyone knew where he stood. Often he could do nothing: as with Jeffrey Baines, who lost an eye merely by using the grindstone without goggles, and then three years later lost the other eye the same way. The goggles were there and Clyde had plagued him to wear them; but still when he saw Baines tapping the pavement, his lifted face bewildered and empty, it tore Clyde. When such things happened he felt a pain of helplessness that changed his nature. As he grew older, and had a family at home, he came to see that he was the father of the shop. For all the trials, he couldn't not work, and he couldn't stop himself getting pleasure from it.

So his life passed, absorbed from day to day, for two decades in which he didn't ask where, further, it was going. But his brain and his hands slowed; he nodded after lunch, and wrote off the early afternoon. He held the drawings away from him and blinked at them: he would sooner die than wear glasses, but the platers joked that he was running out of arm. And by a certain starch of going-on-his-dignity when his men got too chatty, he made it clear that he expected more respect. New machines came into the shop that worked in different ways from the old machines, and seemed a different kind of creature, not human. The old machines were part of his family: he saw them as extensions of the human hand, and as part and parcel of the men who worked them—he saw Strachey in the gnawed twisted drill-bits chucked away, and Dawson in shining wheels turning smoothly. But the new machines rebuffed him: they stayed foreign and filled him with distrust.

The years passed, and he was fighting a shadowy battle with an adversary he could not see: the enemy clung on behind him, getting a soft tight grip on his limbs and joints, and from being as light as air it started to weigh on his back and bend it. Slowly the invisible hands, the many invisible graspers of the spider, tightened on his legs, his hands, tightened on each supple finger like small nooses snagging on the finger-joints and jamming them: but so slowly, crawlingly, without a sound, invisibly, except that he was aware of the thickening of soft cobweb across his eyes, gathering in his body and brain, clogging his thickening blood.

Yet he felt it was not time within, in his seizing blood, that wore him down, but time without, the accelerating business of the world, the way everything had to be done faster, and machinery had got too complicated, and the whole process was out of all control, mad, running amok. But he was a keen hale fighter: after faltering, he came to, and picked up courage. He drove himself hard, and worked doubly hard to understand the new machines.

So braced, he was almost glad when his enemy at last came out into the open: which now it did in a small squad of buff-tunicked men. The Time Study had arrived, and he knew at once they were at war.

'We decided, if it's all right by you, we'd kick off in the Plate Shop,' Strudwick, the Works Manager, told him. A Yorkshireman, with brusque tact he threw in, 'It's the biggest shop by far, it's only fair you get first shot.' He drilled Clyde confidently with his small clear grey eyes, and was staggered when Clyde took umbrage. 'Is my shop slow, then?'

Manly hurt in a manly face. 'Of course it's not slow, Edward.

'I don't see how—' each word underlined with a levelled finger—'my men can work faster, and still do good work.'

The sparkling shirt edged back from the oily prodding. 'Look at it this way, Edward. What will go up with the system won't be speed as such, but productivity.'

Heavy misgiving; but a new zest in a springy manager, and a manly voice was firmly soothing. 'Edward, Edward, give it a try, do—it'll take nothing of the running the shop away from you, it'll just take some of the worry out of it.'

'Who's worried?' A resigned shrug.

Clyde knew what the Scheme meant: each job would be given a set time, and the man doing it would be paid a bonus for the time he saved. The times would be generous, so that no one was demoralized and everyone's greed was kept healthy. It would hurry the men in a bad way, and lead to bad work. But the shop was his, after all; he could do what he liked to any Scheme.

Management, however, had still to recruit Time's army. Presently a stout young apoplectic Consultant was to be seen everywhere in the works: himself a living proof of what Time Study could achieve, for he had gone far for a man under forty, and was built and lined like a man over fifty. He ordained that the scheme would be the special responsibility of Ray Forbes, the Production Controller, the Works Manager's immediate deputy, also an energetic man, and decent; the scheme would be housed in the office next to Forbes. As to staffing, the Consultant, the Works Manager and Forbes put their heads together. Two men from the shop-floor, and two men from the Drawing Office-administrative side, was the Consultant's idea: and on each side an older, experienced man to give weight, and a younger ardent man to give push.

The older men were no problem. In the Plate Shop there was a lithe brisk welder, a little quick monkey of a man with sinews and hair like steel wire: a wizened caustic Australian, Ted, who had exhausted jobs the world over, and was thought sharp as a razor. He was liked to ecstasy by the platers because his soul was as dry and parched as the desert of salt that would deposit from an evaporated ocean. When the Consultant found that the idea of working on the Time Study just gave the welder a crinkle of ironic humour that meant he would be interested in the money, he came back to Forbes beaming. The welder was the man, there was a face you could strike a match on, there was a face to stand over a stop-watch.

And in the Drawing Office there was Bert Cherry. The firm had spent money on Bert Cherry, not because he was a prodigy, but because he, and an advanced training scheme, were in the same place at the same time. In the faith that talent like everything else could be manufactured, he was put through floor work in every workshop, was financed through university and endowed with executive groomings. But at the end of it all there was no executive job going, and no one knew what to do with him. So he was left a senior draughtsman; he did not exert himself to join another firm, for he felt he owed it to his patrons to stay, and moreover it was a comfortable berth in which to drowse. He rotted on the bough. Years of not happy but cushioned relaxation hadn't been the best qualification for executive labours now: but he stood there a live and breathing considerable investment, and the Time Study was the ideal pigeon-hole, found at last, in which to pop him. After all, the platers distrusted the technical side, and it would be no bad thing for them to deal with someone as unformidable and reassuring as Bert Cherry, who could still blind them with science if he chose.

So, for the seniors: they were approached, and were ironically pursed, and sleepily perturbed, respectively, and, respectively, they said Yes. For the juniors, it was not so clear-cut. But they picked a young fitter, Earl Kerry: the fitters rated higher than the platers. Also a young draughtsman, Barry Spurrier, who had come on well in the Drawing Office but aspired to be more than a draughtsman. He had been a buddy of the fitter's in his spell of floor work, so the scheme could start with a rapport, not a rift, between its younger blue and its younger white collar.

The four were installed in a light office next to Forbes's: they were lectured by the Consultant, and equipped with small hardboard palettes, time-sheets, stop-watches, slide-rules, and an inexhaustible supply of biros.

Thus loaded and primed, they were fired off at the shop. Clyde was lying in wait.

12

The first study was taken by the Australian: this was a shrewd idea of Forbes's, for the Australian was the toughest nut there. And that study went well. Clyde passed only once, nodding curtly, 'Morning Ted', making it clear that he took just the tone he would use if Ted were still working under him.

The next study was taken by Bert Cherry, who puffed himself out and proceeded with a stateliness, in a spotless white tunic like a chemist's which he had bought specially, and which delighted the platers. With a good deal of affable confusion as to what went where in the job and in the study, in an odd mixture of bossing and chatting, he got through, the plater getting rather his own way as to speed. Clyde hovered in the distance, but only to advertise that he took no interest: he even seemed not to see the plumped white brilliance.

For the third study, taken by Barry Spurrier, Clyde drew closer: he followed it with interest, saying nothing and clinking dangerously. And in the fourth study, taken by the fitter, Earl Kerry, he continually intervened. He talked to the plater; he talked to the fitter; he disagreed with Kerry on the time; he wondered whether his stop-watch was really on the dot, he took it, and seemed in danger of showing his genius for repair there and then. The study broke down in a shambles: Kerry and Clyde came to words, but youth was no match for authority, and was shouted from the Plate Shop.

So Earl's study was useless, and the Time Study was alerted as to Clyde. But after that set-to, Clyde was annoyed with himself, and kept his distance. And after the first couple of weeks, he got used to them; they were always there and studying, but nothing seemed to come of it. It made his blood boil, to see one of his burly giants of platers being stop-watched by an office-pale youth from the Drawing Office. But he despised them too much to be alarmed.

Time passed, and the studies accumulated. It once seemed impossible to the four men that they should ever get their minds round all the operations that went forward in the shop. Yet presently they knew how long the whole performance took, for all the embellishments and diversions slipped in by the hostile plater. They knew how long it took to queue at the Drawing Stores and bang on the counter; how long to flap open a drawing like a tent being difficult, to get it the right way up, to not make head or tail of it, to aggravate the brain by scratching the head, then to glimmer, to glow, to blaze with understanding; to search out the wrong ruler, fumble with the unnecessary set-square, and dash the right steel ruler down on the metal with a musical bang; to scratch with a scriber or drag a chalk line of five, of ten, of fifteen feet; to chuck the metal on a trolley, to haggle with Trout, to lug it down the gang-way and tip it out by the shears; to slice through thick iron like hot butter, to fold it like paper, to curl it like ringlets, to hole it like a colander, when it was sixteenth, quarter or three-eighths thick; to take it to the smith, have it redden, whiten, dazzle in the fire, and explode in meteors as it squelched and stretched under the sledge; how long to take the whole caboodle down the fitters', to weld it and bolt it and rivet it whole; how long to spray it with a red toxic cloud; how long to tow it away and leave it at the Dump; and how long to sigh, and have a fag, and trail up the shop, screw up the bits of drawing, and lob them in over the counter at surly Len Petchey.

The times for all these things the time-studiers knew, or at least they had them filed. They had reached the point where they could officially prescribe times for new work that went through the shop. Bert Cherry had the first such job, and with some nervous taking of deep breaths, and some sluggish awakening of dormant gift, he broke down the manufacture of a whole machine, made out a separate card for each operation, and assigned it a time. A batch of green job-cards was paper-clipped to the bottom of each large buff master-sheet, and the whole stack of these was taken up to Clyde by Forbes himself, and explained. The procedure was very simple: each green card was to be given to the man doing that job, and the cards were to be given out in the order they were in, so the work went through smoothly from start to finish.

But this principle, which seemed so clear to Forbes, was opaque to Clyde. Evidently there was something elusive, subtle, deceptive, in the very seeming simplicity of it. Forbes spent a long time explaining, and Clyde followed every word with listening eyes: and yet it appeared at the end that on Clyde's lucid mechanical genius a thin foggy cloud had descended, somewhere he had lost the thread, and Forbes had to start again. Forbes persisted. Clyde had sincere doubts; but if Mr Forbes was sure he should give these new cards a try in his shop, well, he would give them a try.

And a trial, in some sense, Clyde did give the cards. He received the new buff master-cards into his safekeeping, and the green cards were distributed. But in a curious way these cards seemed to get all over the shop, and to turn up in the unlikeliest places. They had a mischievous life of their own, they would dance out of the driller's hands into the welder's when there was no welding to be done. They burrowed deep in Clyde's trouser pockets, and try as he might to reach down and locate them, it was no go, they screwed themselves up, and nestled and hid beneath the screwdrivers and bolts. They crept into the little drawers of his office, and concealed themselves in wads of old work-sheets: one made for the window, and took a gust to a neighbouring roof. Clyde followed all this in helpless bewilderment: it seemed like the undoing of Pandora's box. But let management not worry, Clyde would cope: he told each man what to do, and the actual machinery went through like clockwork. Few of the platers knew what time they were on for it. Never mind, they would be paid under the old scheme, no harm done.

The next set of cards went the same way, and the next. But Clyde knew that management, and the men promised a bonus, would stand only so much, and, keeping one move ahead of the mounting exasperation, he slipped the green cards into effect. What this would mean for him was still not clear, but it became clear. He spent his time giving out cards, and if there were any queries or problems, the platers went to the Time Study office: Clyde was cut out. But then, if the men did come to him in difficulties, he blamed the trouble on the Time Study, and sent them round there: he drove them into the Time Study's fold, and left himself more exposed.

The flow of cards increased stealthily, till it was obvious to Clyde that he could only slow the enemy, he could not win. In these still early days, in his own shop, he felt like a man trapped in a closed space while the rising water crept up the wall. So he went on the attack, and every time a time-study was done in the shop, he would sooner or later go over and act out the little obstructive inspirations that came to him. He had never before been in the situation of regularly trying to damage or spoil: it kept him in a permanent burning irritation with himself and with everyone else. His war with the Time Study became the thing he was most interested in. And all the time the Study drove him back, till it was clear to everyone that he was exasperated, and ageing fast, and losing his touch. He grew clumsier with the machinery and more bossy with the men, till the platers cursed when they saw him coming, a hungry mole-wrench opening and shutting in his hand. Now he exaggerated the difference in age between his men and himself, and saw in them the slipshod uppish modern type. At the same time he needed now, as he didn't before, a clear show of respect, and he exacted it with his peremptory voice. His inventions came fewer and further between. He got into a groove of fretting and bossing. The older platers were aghast to see it, but then he bossed them, and they lost sympathy.

In such conditions the Plate Shop couldn't work as it did. Perhaps in the past Clyde made thousands for the firm of which scarce a penny trickled through into his pay-packet, but that tide ebbed away on all sides now. And yet for all this he was only surprised and vaguely troubled, when the rumour reached him, and soon it was common knowledge in the works, that every time one of their shares came up on the market, it was bought up by Mundo Tubes of Mexico City. Mexico City? What did Mexico City want with their engineering works? Clyde knew what it meant —the end: yet he couldn't see why it should come to this.

Then something happened that changed his hold on life. He was walking down the gangway late one evening, thinking he had the shop to himself, when a monkey-wrench smashed into the concrete floor right in front of him. It had fallen from the roof. He moved his foot back involuntarily, for his first thought was that it had just missed crushing his foot. Immediately afterwards, he realized it had just missed his head. The entire shop quivered. There was a shadowy vibration on the catwalk, he wasn't sure if he heard a soft sniggering laugh. He ran to the nearest ladder, but then heard a great clatter of boots on steel at the far end of the shop. He ran up there, and dodged round the machinery. Perhaps he heard a momentary scuffling, but he found no-one, the shop was empty. He knew now that one of his men hated him enough to kill him casually. He looked round his shop with different eyes, there was no knowing who it might be.

The wrench went into his pocket with other gadgets, and stayed there. Sometimes, when hard-pressed, his hand closed on it meditatively. His loathing of the Time Study concentrated.

13

It was a remarkable thing that though, in the past, with every job the men did, they grounded on unforeseen rocks and reefs, and cried perpetually to Clyde for aid, now that the Time Study was introduced the problems mysteriously disappeared, the rocks and reefs sank away to the ocean floor, and everything sailed smoothly—except that for this drilling, that marking out, the other strip of welding, the time allowed just wasn't enough. The time ran away like water, or devalued like inflating money, so that a job that took an hour last week took an hour and ten minutes this. For the Time Study had brought in a new currency, and was a mint and bank of time: it stood on vast deposits of time's sand that could be mined and shoveled out by the minute or the day to platers who constantly came with hour-glasses running out, broken, mysteriously flawed and cracked so somehow the sand just slid away unseen. And surely the sands were golden, for the time was money, but of this elusive new currency Clyde's pockets were bare. He loitered outside the bank like an exasperated bankrupt, watching his men scramble in and out, and emerge sometimes contented and sleek, their job-cards fattened by biro corrections, and sometimes venting frosty blasts of abuse, but always with their thoughts centered on the office, while he, Clyde, stood by, the poor man driving no trade, with no hours to buy nor seconds to sell. He was shouldered out, displaced, and each of the time-studiers could feel that he stood there secure as the fourth part of a Foreman.

But sand runs and what reserves had that bank? While so much was firmly under way and the Time Study was starting to bite, news came that Mundo Tubes, that now owned nearly half the shares in the firm, had insisted on joining the board. He could not be kept off it, and presently he was no longer in Mexico City but in England, and not only in England but in the works, sequestered with management and patrolling the shops. He was not visibly scorched by the Mexican sun, and it appeared also he was not strictly Spanish: his surname was O'Hara, a short plump freckled man with ruffled grey hair. There was an assurance, a smack of wealth somewhere there, but he was an anticlimax and was not taken seriously. It was appreciated that he took an interest in the firm. And an interest he did take, he was always dropping in on little visits and management couldn't keep track of him. It transpired later there was no official in the firm with whom he had not hobnobbed, and not a paper in the offices he had not scanned—just while working himself in.

Then new news broke: he had been, and he had gone. He had sold up his interest to Mackworth Crowley. Mackworth Crowley owned many things across the world, and in particular they owned Exells, the mammoth steel and engineering combine that was the factory's main rival. It appeared they had also picked up certain stray shares that had come on the market before Mundo Tubes came into play. In his brief English life, O'Hara had written up his findings: and these files too, there was a weight of them, slipped into the hands of Mackworth Crowley.

The taken-over factory waited in paralysis. The shop stewards were active, but nothing was clear. Word filtered down that everything was to continue just as it was: there would be an invisible takeover in the higher stratosphere, affecting the floor-worker not at all except that he might soon get more money; though it was also said that Crowley had a plan by which everything would be smashed and sold up, and all of them flung out of work. But life proceeded as though this could never happen—even though everyone felt also that they sat together on a long branch slowly tearing from the trunk.

Clyde wondered whether anything could happen to him. He couldn't imagine it, he knew too much. He so much was the Plate Shop that unless Mackworth Crowley sold up everything for scrap, they would have to keep him on. And here he saw a ray of light: Mackworth Crowley would have their own schemes and recipes for production control, and possibly the Time Study was more at risk than he was. Perhaps, oh perhaps, Forbes and his merry men hung by a thread. Perhaps unlooked-for help had come, and he could sweep them from his shop. He accelerated his efforts against them, as though when he got rid of them, he could call the shop his own.

14

What form the possible Apocalypse might take, no one knew. But one morning the first men into the works were surprised to see that beside the Plate Shop, a large caravan had appeared: light, silvery, shining in the dusty yard. There was nothing on it to say what it was.

'Oi, oi, we got the diddicoys in?' a plater called. An apprentice sang out, 'Gypo-roady!'

The caravan door was open, and whoever used it was evidently well under way with his day's work. There were papers spread over a desk. While they stood there, a man behind them said 'Morning' in a nondescript voice, and passed between them into the caravan. He was a man in his forties, not marked in feature, in the grey trousers of a suit, and in a quiet distinct check shirt. The platers were inclined to ask who the hell he was, but he was too absorbed in his papers. They stared at him a little, to make it clear they saw him as an interloper, then drew off.

Everyone coming to work that morning saw the caravan and wondered; but who was in it, no one knew. Yet while the question smouldered through the works, the answer to it came not slowly but like fire in a gale, so that in half an hour there was not an office-girl or labourer who did not know that the invasion had occurred, and that not accountants had come, not teams of emissaries, but that in the small caravan in the heart of the works was the man they expected never to see. He was too far removed, too high, at the centre of his hundred firms, hooped round by directors and bankers, flanked and supported by accountants and managers and disinterested public men—that in the caravan was Austin Crowley, the acting head of Mackworth Crowley.

It did appear that he had brought four secretaries with him: they were hidden away in an office he had commandeered. Crowley himself was based in the caravan, but was seldom there in the daytime. From bright dawn when the first day-worker arrived, to smoky dusk when the last man left, the caravan stood empty and Crowley was somewhere in the works. The men working nights found that Crowley worked nights. They couldn't work out when he slept, or did anything else.

For some time he was occupied in the offices. Then, one morning, he walked into the Plate Shop. And just as though indeed he rode in enthroned on a silver chariot strewn with silks, to the heavy chink of gold trappings, while ranked executives cast rosepetals and gossamer before him: behold thou are fair, my fortune: just so, the raised arms descended, the machines faltered and stopped, a huge silence expanded through the shop, and all eyes turned on Crowley. Crowley seemed aware and unaware of this: he was not embarrassed. He flitted lightly up the steps into Clyde's office, and for a long time neither he nor the Foreman reappeared. If the platers hesitantly went in, they invariably found Clyde holding forth in his familiar style, punctuated by sharp brief questions from Crowley which he answered without always seeing the point of them.

Crowley was handsome and slim. He evidently exercised and was vain of his figure; he kept well in view a more than English suntan, and a quiet high expensiveness showed in the keen line of his trousers. His eyes however were so intent that meeting them was like being nipped by small pincers. Clyde gradually realized that the fierceness of this look was the fierceness of the tension Crowley was in, as he rigidly restrained his biting impatience with the rambling and irrelevance in Clyde's long answers. Crowley never relaxed his staccato courtesy.

Clyde took Crowley on a tour of the shop, and the roisterous platers were subdued when he got to them. Even 'Lias Trigg, who in honour of his name had resurrected, for performance when Crowley just hove in sight at the far end of the shop, the enormous squawking cock-crow he had used to project from the back row of the cinema when the Pathé news came on, only rolled his eyes and was blood-out-of-a-stone when Crowley accosted him.

Crowley continued round the works, and only the occasional remark from him caused alarm. He observed in passing to Forbes, the Production Controller, that he had noticed that he always came in to work at the same time each morning, and Forbes momentarily felt the knife-edge kiss his skin. But in general he seemed understanding. The shop stewards found him surprisingly reasonable, considering his reputation. He told them that Mackworth Crowley were already in communication with the union head office.

Within two weeks he left, and took the caravan with him. Evidently he had learnt all he needed to know, and the factory waited to hear his decision.

In the meantime, day-to-day transactions went forward as usual, and local quarrels continued as though they had years to go. The only difference was the presence, almost in the air of the shop, of a confused anxiety that everyone felt. A pressure of concern was transmitted down all the pecking lines, and built up at the ends. The labourers were treated more like dogs, old Len Petchey in the Drawing Stores was more badgered and harassed. And in all the workings of the firm there was less oil and more friction, more clashing of cross-purposes.

It was so for Clyde; then a day came when nothing would comply with him any more. He had had one of his best ideas, which would save a machine that otherwise would be useless. And in reward for this he had accidents in his shop, a foreigner whom he had specially favoured shouted in his face, and his oldest buddy of all, George Reynolds, had come to see him just for the purpose of making trouble. It was too much, too much, he had to chuck Reynolds out. But as Reynolds left, something inside him quaked or gave, and as though all the strain of these years condensed at once, the pain in his body turned to a fearful wrench and tearing as though his lungs had been filled with lead and someone was trying to rip up his chest and rip them out. Something terrible had hold of him, he couldn't breathe, he was afraid.

The claw on him relaxed, he was left shakily on his feet, restlessly exhausted, saying over and over, 'What possessed the man?'

15

Clyde had seldom gone into the Time Study Office, but he had its number: a sterile bank of adding-machines, where busy machine-men talked rapidly in numbers. But no one time-studied the time-studiers, and if Clyde could have seen their office in the late, stale time of the afternoon, when the very air was hot, dried-out and dead, he would have thought that Time itself had come to a standstill there. The eternity of job-times and man-hours were shut up in two flaked and rusted filing cabinets. There were three calendars on the wall—they showed giant screw-gauges radiant on hillocks of velvet, or, more subtly, heathery glens with toolmakers' brand-names modestly loitering in the corners—but the calendars didn't agree, and all lagged months in the rear. The time-studiers themselves were rapt and still. Bert Cherry sat with his soft stoutness collapsed on itself, and the white ammonia prints spread round him like petals of a fat pungent flower. His blue eyes never moved. Even his pipe had gone out, though he still sleepily munched it like a baby asleep at the bottle. The fragrant honey-sweet cloud of smoke staled round him in thinning wreathes.

Through the thin hardboard walls came the muffled sound of the hooter for tea-break, and only then did the drowsed office stir. Di splashed in with a large tin jug of tea, and a Cellophane packet of biscuits for Bert Cherry. The stationery cupboard slouched when she opened it to take out the crockery, and stood bolt upright again with a loud tinny crash when she slammed it. Earl Kerry got out his comb, and the war comic he kept in his desk. Ted, the Australian, said, ''Ere, 'ere, the little bud unfolds,' as Bert Cherry sat a little up, and started to screw his face up and blink.

Ted put his feet up on the tin waste-paper box, hunched his lithe body, and started absorbedly hewing and whittling a pencil down to the stub, and reminiscing. The accident this morning recalled to him other industrial accidents he had seen across the world, and Barry and Earl Kerry listened bemused as it seemed there would be no end to the calm catalogue of fingers shot off by rivet-guns, feet descended on by girders, bodies caught, divided and mangled in every kind of iron horror. This took him soon to the war — but he had enjoyed the war, he had seen the world. In the quiet office, in the quiet pleasant pause in the afternoon, the time-studiers only slipped backwards in time, and basked with Ted on consecutive beaches, as he moved on with the troops while the Japanese came island-hopping behind him. The yellow shavings from his whittling twizzled down like cast seeds, and landed with a soft patter in the tin.

So, till the distant hooter sounded the end of tea-break, and promptly, not a moment lost, there was a barbaric clump on the door, and with hardly a pause 'Lias Trigg and Nutty Saville, the two inseparables, shuffled in, as it were touching their forelocks, with a pretended diffidence such as might overwhelm them in entering something between a church and a police station. They made a bee-line for Bert Cherry.

'Wup, 'Lias!' 'Been over-timed then, 'Lias, do you want to

give some back?' 'Tell us a good'n, 'Lias,' the time-studiers cried, 'Lias Trigg being a public figure.

But 'Lias Trigg was not the man he had been, evidently bad experiences had worn him down: he looked thinner, he stooped a little, and as he walked gravely forward he turned on the time-studiers a wistful eye, reproachful but mild. He said to Bert Cherry in a voice crumbling with trouble,

'Oh, Mr Cherry, I don't know what it is. I tried my best but I just can't meet this time.' In a final gesture of helplessness he let go of his green job-cards, so they tumbled on Bert Cherry's desk.

'Well, old chap, don't worry, we'll soon see about this,' Cherry said, and he picked up the tickets. While he scrutinized them, 'Lias just summoned the courage to look round plaintively, and he gave a look especially wounded and pleading to Ted, whose own returning face was a study in wizened leather.

Eventually Cherry rose to his feet, puffing out clouds of sweet tobacco. 'Sorry old chap, you've got as much there as you can have. Not a chance of any more, couldn't do it, old boy, no.'

The two platers stood crestfallen, a heartrending picture. Barry could hardly believe it: Trigg opened his mouth, and out crept a little lost rustle of a voice, evidently copied with care from Bowditch, the profile burner. 'I don't know how I can cope, Mr Cherry.'

Cherry was tender-hearted, he came over flushed and embarrassed, 'Oh well now, come along now, don't talk like that. How's that boy of yours getting along, eh?'

But 'Lias Trigg's boy was far from well: Barry did not know what impression Cherry was under, but he did know 'Lias's boy, who was taller than 'Lias and an apprentice blacksmith. But Cherry's tobacco-smoke churned and thickened as though it would condense and rain brown tears. 'Oh, what bad luck. Oh dear. How long did you say the job took? Fifty minutes? Not a chance, couldn't do it, more than my life's worth. Could you do it in thirty?'

'I'd—try, Mr Cherry,' from plaintive 'Lias.

'Give me the ticket,' Cherry said, virile and energetic, and scribbled vigorously on it. Trigg picked it up gratefully, and herded his other tickets together: then, sharply, like soldiers changing guard, he stepped back and Saville stepped forward.

Cherry looked at him, nonplussed. 'Well, Nutty, what's the problem?'

They all jumped, as Saville bellowed out loud in his strongest indignation, 'It's the Jib Guards, Mr Cherry!'

'The Jib Guards, Nutty? What's wrong with them?'

'What's wrong with them?!' Saville glared round at everyone, paralysed with outrage.

'Well, let's have a look at them. Got the drawing?'

'Of course!' However, there followed a long delay, while Saville reached down into his pockets, and groped; eventually little bits and scraps of paper started to emerge, and then a large crumpled wad, that he shook out in tatters on to Cherry's desk. With ardour he pieced them together, while Cherry sat puffing his pipe and dazedly gazing as the parts and elevations of the Jib Guards materialized before his eyes. Trigg, with his bright eyes half-closed as if in pain, drew up at Saville's elbow, ready to arbitrate.

As Saville was ready to launch, however, Ray Forbes, the Production Controller, the whole factory's third-in-command, darted in, and the time-studiers jumped again. The Time Study was his special province, his own office was next door. He came in so briskly that he seemed already through the door before it snapped open, and when he stopped there was a pause as if he had to catch up with himself before he spoke. He invariably wore a spotless, newly-pressed navy suit; his sharp-featured, intelligent face, always cleanly shaved and very washed, had a pale shine. At the sight of Trigg and Saville his face pleasantly sharpened. 'Why, hello. I hear you're short of a driller in the Plate Shop.'

'How's that?' 'Come again?' the platers said.

'I said, I hear Clyde has given Pethick the sack.'

'Oh, Pevvick,' they said, not interested.

'Well, you don't seem too cut up.'

Saville was amazed at the question. 'He wasn't one of us, was he?'

Trigg inquired, *sotto voce*, of Saville, 'What *is* he, when he's at home, Nutty?' and they continued, oblivious of the office,

'Search me, 'Lias.'

'No, but I mean—he's not a *Russian*, is he?'

All Saville's indignation flared again, 'A Russian, 'Lias?!'

''Ungarian, is he? Pole? He's from out that way.'

'Oh, well, if he's from out that way, that would be it then, wouldn't it, 'Lias?'

They fell silent.

Forbes extracted the details of what had happened, then asked, 'How do you rate him, as a driller?'

Saville said at once, stridently, 'Not much cop, Mr Forbes!' but Trigg demurred, 'Go on, Nutty. Pevvick was a good driller.'

Saville reconsidered, then said with energy 'Yes, yes, when you think about it, Mr Forbes—he was a good driller.'

Trigg added, 'He'd drill a hole clean as a whistle. And I never known him break a bit, not through being cack-handed.'

Saville nodded. 'He's right, he's right. Not once.'

'Not like Eric Strachey, eh, Nutty?'

'Strachey! Oh God, Strachey!'

'I reckon Strachey chews bits and spits brown—the holes he sends you, on the skew, mucky at the edges. Oo-er, I've had some narsty holes from Strachey.'

Saville nodded with emphasis, but then thought further. 'Still, wouldn't you say, 'Lias, when he gets his finger out, Strachey's a good driller too?'

'I suppose he is really, Nutty, when you think about it.'

'He is, 'Lias! Oh yes, he's very expert, Eric Strachey.'

'He is expert.'

'They're both good drillers really.' Saville nodded, and the two platers smiled with unanimity.

'He's a good old boy, Strachey,' Trigg added. 'He crowned me with a monkey-wrench, once. I saw stars for bloody years!'

Ted leaned forward at his desk. 'Ah, I wondered what had caused it.'

'Come again, darling.' Trigg grinned.

Saville and Trigg conferred, then Trigg said, 'Will that be all, Mr Forbes? I don't want to lose none of this here precious *time* what Mr Cherry give me.'

Saville collected his drawing and stuffed it into his pockets, and the two platers shuffled out, evidently preferring to haggle with Cherry when Forbes wasn't there.

Forbes put his elbows up on the shelf behind him and leaned back. He was in his confiding afternoon mood. 'That man again! What a curse Clyde is! '

'Oh, he's a tartar,' Earl Kerry chimed.

'But what'll happen to Pethick?' Barry Spurrier asked, his voice tense with sudden concern.

Ted and Earl Kerry exchanged looks: they had seen Barry out with Pethick's daughter.

'Don't worry, Barry,' Earl said. 'He's seen Hawkins, and there's a union meeting today, after work. He'll be back at his drill tomorrow.'

'You think they'll make something of it, Earl?' Forbes smiled: his eyes were bright, he had an interest in the issue.

Ted remarked, 'They can do what they like, Clyde won't back down. If they push him, he'll say, "Pethick goes, or I go."' Then he paused, took in the implication of what he had just said, and his face went quizzical. He added, to Forbes, 'He'll expect Management to back him.'

'He'll expect it, Ted. But I don't see that we can have good men sacked out of hand, just like that. Should we back him?'

Then all the time-studiers nodded, and smiled, and saw in the distance hope, and the chance to finish Clyde. So much trouble he had given them, and he would not easily be dislodged; he knew the in and out of everything in the shop, and all the platers walked in his shadow. Also Stacey, the General Manager, liked Clyde and would want to keep him. But now if the union dug its heels in, and so did Clyde, and then a managerial inquiry was launched, and found out that the sacking of Pethick was just intolerable bullying and caprice of the kind Clyde went in for all the time now: then as Clyde, under attack, deepened in obstinacy, the great wave would burst and smash him.

Bert Cherry woke to the main point, and murmured in his reverie, 'Dawson would make as good a foreman as Clyde, any day.'

Forbes nodded. 'Dawson would be very good.' He spoke with a quiet inward emphasis, and in the office there was a short tense silence of shared hope.

Forbes looked at his watch. 'I must go—Stacey's up in London, Strudwick's off this afternoon, so I've got the Grand Turk all to myself!' He sparkled, at the thought of this exotic buyer, coming now to visit the works. 'Ah well,' said Ted, 'We'll keep Di on a short tether.' Forbes smiled at the office-girl in a friendly way. Then he took off, his jacket-tails flew up, and the brisk friendly nod he gave them in leaving seemed to hover in the air, and tip towards them amiably, after his door had closed. Ted's ironic brow went up; Bert Cherry shivered in the draught of such haste; Barry Spurrier, who admired Forbes, was as always braced by his speed, and sat taller.

Barry, Ted, Earl and Di all left on various studies and errands. Bert Cherry, left to himself, lit up again and repaired the rich sweet honey-smelling envelope of pipe-smoke he liked to have all round him. For contrast, he took the corner of an ammonia-print, crumpled the crisp paper so it crackled nicely, and inhaled with pleasure the faint scent of ammonia that still clung to it. Then there was a slow shifting and subsidence through all his warm frame, and the office fell silent, except that through the wall behind him, just, came a muffled continuous din, like a city outside for ever falling to pieces.

*

Beneath his crispness Forbes was anxious as he walked quickly to the works gate. With the shadow of Crowley hanging over the factory, they needed to sell every machine they could and win every possible order. He worried also that the Turk might know the trouble they were in, and force down the price. It was too bad of Stacey and Strudwick, leaving him to handle this on his own.

The Turk proved to be, not corpulence and a fez, but a

lean, slightly stooping, elegantly weary man, who, as they strolled towards the workshops, confided that his great pleasure in England was in going to Kew Gardens. If he knew anything of the factory's troubles, he gave no sign, and Forbes relaxed as they wound through the various workshops, and then crossed to the ranks of new mixers in the yard: mixers bright vermilion, bright yellow, clear sky-blue. In the vivid late-afternoon light, they sauntered among the brilliant colours as though they were in just such a garden as the Turk loved. But this was Forbes's garden, and he dwelt tenderly on the details of his new machines.

The Turk's brown eyes rested patiently on Forbes, and he listened with interest although these innovations were not so fresh. He scanned Forbes's navy suit, well-cut and well-pressed, without elegance, without chic. The white shirt and dark tie must have been chosen with never the least thought of a woman. He looked from the well-polished, plain black shoes to the pale sharp face, alert, intent, shrewd; without urbanity; where pleasure, if it had passed, had passed without trace. And yet he preferred Forbes to the coarseness of pleasure, the stylelessness, of the jolly type of English manager. He liked Forbes: Forbes was obviously honest and dedicated. Yet also Amil was touched with pity. He was a much-travelled man, he thought of Germany and Japan, and—how could these jog-along English factories think they would compete?

The Turk wanted to buy, Forbes wanted to sell, but the price the Turk offered was shockingly low. Forbes was stuck, anxiety grew. Did the Turk know about Crowley? The Turk looked on with amused sympathy, thinking only: poor English, they want to bargain, but they don't know how. He did not hurry. His long blade of nose peered into a mixer-bowl. He slapped the side of a motor, and rested on the wheel a slender shoe, all coloured flanges and overlaps of peppered and lacy leather.

A light switched on in Forbes's head. 'We do give various discounts, for quantity . . .'

The Turk seized, 'And for currency-change, and . . .'

Discounts, discounts were the way. Under the cover of elusive sliding discounts that Forbes's ingenuity supplied, they haggled: and they agreed.

Bland and pleased together, they strolled back across the wide sunlit yard, at a distance from the plain grey bulk of the Plate Shop. The featureless grey shed was so long, it extended from side to side of their sight: it lay like a dead snake across the ground. Half way down its length, the side-doors were open, there was blackness and teeming smoke inside, and deafening noise. But they were removed from it, treading easily across the concrete plain, with its tufts of grass and dandelion. Among the lined lorries near the gate, two apprentices and a plater, truants from the Plate Shop, played football. They punted the ball, it sailed high into the air and caught the sun like an orange star. Forbes reflected that Stacey and Strudwick had not been needed after all, they would probably have been in the way.

They chatted intermittently. Forbes liked the Turk with his odd taste for horticulture. And the Turk liked Forbes, he was touched by the picture he had formed of these English gentlemen-managers, telling the truth while their ship went down.

16

The closing hooter wailed over the steaming factory, and the
din in the workshops faltered and dropped, leaving the ring
of steel downed on concrete, the crunching tramp of boots,
and the low ripple of sporadic talk. Through the open doors
at the end of the shop, the rusty late-afternoon sunlight
poured in, and died slowly in the hanging smoke and dust. It
sprinkled a hot cinnamon dapple on the machinery, and
pointed, in burning copper red, so they stood out like small
sooty flames, the oil-mottled faces and hands of the men: as,

in gangs and handfuls and singly, exhausted but relaxing, they trooped out through the brown haze like live embers, black and red, raked from an opened furnace.

The air outside was briefly sweet, then, with a quick coughing, a stampede of cars, scooters, choppers and bikes rounded the side of the shop like a released flood, burst on the crowd of walking men, and then person and vehicle, shouts, dust and exhaust, were all stirred together in one weary churning turmoil that gradually drove to the main gates. There was a momentary arrest at the road, but then a scooter and a bike, and a thread of men, dodged across, and the heavy traffic had no option but to wait, droning and throbbing, till the factory was cleared.

Pethick stood near the canteen, watching the men leave. The pleasant tired evening release was so much what had happened at the end of every day for years that he could hardly believe he might not know it again. With old affection he watched George Reynolds, his cap lugged down over his eyes, advancing ponderously through the walking men, bolt upright on his sit-up-and-beg bicycle.

His buddy Wally Reed came to join him, and they went into the canteen, where the union meeting would be. All the tables had been stacked against the walls, except for one at the end of the room, and the chairs were arranged in rough lines; to everything clung the faint unpleasant smell of old cooking. There was no crowd. The strong, relaxed backs of half-a-dozen platers rose from the rippling lines of chair-backs like lonely rocks in a dead sea. At the back of the room, the three men who were the union, Riley, Marlow, and Hawkins the Shop Steward, rocked their chairs inwards, and chatted assuredly in low voices. Near the front, 'Lias Trigg expanded on an accident he had had with a rivet-gun, and raised for public inspection a large boot, scuffed down one side, with the foot still inside it that had been miraculously preserved. Reg Barrett, who worked the brake press, sat near him nodding and not listening, urgently scanning the results in the evening paper.

Pethick went cold inside. He had imagined a crowded room, a tense meeting, but all that happened for the present was that two platers shouted across the room at intervals,

'Is old Hopper coming?'

'Dunno.'

'Hopper's an arse.'

There was soft laughter at the back of the room, and Hawkins, Riley and Marlow started to filter through the chairs to the front. Hawkins was a young Shop Steward, only thirty-six: but in the event he had minded his p's and q's and given nothing away, and was thought not a write-off. He moved forward at his leisure, in a certain demureness of importance. Pethick looked with distrust at the sleek way he had creamed his thinning hair over his scalp. He was disgusted with the platers who had come, because so many others had stayed away.

The other platers, substantial men, ignored Hawkins and talked on desultorily but loudly, so the meeting should start at their pleasure, not his.

Hawkins called the meeting to order, but he had barely dispatched the minutes when there was a loud banging at the back of the room. Someone was trying to open the door the wrong way. Then the door bounded open, and a large broad plater in a thick navy donkey-jacket heaved in, and, apparently unconscious there was anyone there, turned round and slammed the door deliberately and with force. The platers puckered to each other, this happened every time. In loud tramping boots the new arrival heaved down the gangway, preoccupied, breathing with a tearing hoarse rasp that it hurt to hear. He laboured past Pethick, ignoring him, but nodded shortly to Reed and sat down on the next chair. Then, he was noisily involved in undoing his donkey-jacket and in re-aligning his chair. He was Hopper; but Hawkins resumed.

Hawkins was scarcely two notices further, however, when 'Lias Trigg raised an arm, kicked the chair in front of him, and called out, 'Point of order, Mr Chairman, point of order!' The platers grinned and chuckled, this also happened every time.

'Mr Chairman, will you take a question, Mr Chairman?'

Hawkins nodded, his face a weary martyrdom. Trigg rolled his bright black eyes, that were like a cow's, and said, 'You got an allotment, don't you?'

Hawkins was nonplussed, 'Yeah . . .'

'Yes! And you flog stuff off it, don't you?'

'Yeah.'

'Well, Mr Chairman, I've got a bone to pick with you!' Trigg looked round the room in exultation. 'Call yourself a Union man? One man, one job, that's what Union is. Isn't it? I mean, my brother Ned, he's got a small-holding, and he's got a stall down the market, and he doesn't want the price brought down by no cheap greens off of allotments, does he? All right, Mr Chairman, point of order, that's all it was.'

Hawkins muttered weakly, 'Open market, i'n'it?' Hopper leaned over to Reed, and his painful breathing turned to a hot wheezing scoff. '*Hor*-kins—he'll never be a big-shot!'

Then there was dead silence, as Hawkins gave the latest information about the takeover and Mackworth Crowley. Hopper's breathing slowed, Trigg's smile seemed merely a residue on his face, even Pethick sat erect with attention.

Hawkins's news, however, was only to the effect that the London office had had several discussions with Crowley, and was well aware of the situation. Head office did not know why the caravan had come back, but they did know that no definite decision had yet been taken. In any case head office was sending someone to make a full study of the factory's situation. He was a most distinguished unionist, he had been knighted. 'We'll make short work of him,' said 'Lias Trigg.

Hawkins proceeded patiently, deadpan, utterly without enthusiasm, to the first piece of business. Barrett, at the brake press, had put the big bend and the little bend at the wrong ends of a consignment of steel bars. When he re-did them, he only got ordinary time: he accepted this at the time, but the next day came to Hawkins demanding bonus money as well. Hawkins saw no chance of it, but he also saw that in talking to Barrett now, he was talking to Mrs Barrett of the night before, and that therefore he had no option but to bring the matter to the meeting, let it go as it would. He made the best case he could, but was himself surprised when, without more ado, the platers voted to go slow if Barrett did not get his bonus.

While this business went forward, Hopper kept coughing in Reed's ear, 'It's like *Hor*-kins to spend half-hour on that . . . this chap, *Hor*-kins, he thinks he's Lord Muck now. You know, Wally. . . . he wants to get into the Buffs . . . He'll never make it.'

'No?'

'Nah! 'sgot no common,' Hopper began—but he couldn't go on, he was shaken in a chain of racking coughs. He worked at a bay in the corner of the Plate Shop, and whenever the door there was open, thin pink or azure clouds hovered in from the Paint Shop next door. Over the years the pretty mist had clogged and rotted his lungs. But except when the cough clutched him by the throat and yanked him under, he refused to think of the damage done, and never mentioned it at union meetings.

When he was bearably recovered, he leaned over again to Reed, and gasped, 'We went once . . . Union Convention . . . London hotel . . . pile on those carpets, Wally—foot deep it was, damn near drowned . . . called the waiter. . . . short for myself . . . Gin Fizz for Jimmy Marlow—well, what do you expect? . . . and I asked *Hor*kins what he wanted . . . and he said, pickled onions!'

Hopper sat back and pulled his shirt wide open. Hawkins, resting a dull, aware eye on Hopper, continued his address while Hopper resumed, 'Next thing . . . *Hor*-kins hollers out, "Cherist, Harry . . . here's a bloody gold-fish bowl!" . . . it was the Johnny with the pickled onions . . . put them down, Jimmy Marlow and me got talking . . . and Jimmy said to me—I'll never forget this, Wally—"Harry," he said . . . "There's *etiquette*!" . . . I looked round, there was *Hor*-kins . . . cheerful as you like . . . arm stretched out . . . and his oily mitt up to the wrist in the bowl of pickled onions! . . . "There's etiquette! " . . . and that's the man, Wally . . . wants to get into the Buffs . . . Werl!' Hopper finished, coughing and hacking, and beamed at Hawkins.

Pethick only half-attended, wondering all the time, when *would* they get to him? Trigg asked a question, but it was mere bumptious prevarication, they were just putting him off. It had steadily come clearer to him that they were going to leave him in the lurch. His eye was caught by the rapid swing of Marlow's foot, under the table, in time to Hawkins' speech. Marlow's eyes were blue and sharp and watched Hawkins keenly as though he knew in advance all he would say. Then Pethick realized—Hawkins was only the front man, Jimmy Marlow was the man who counted, and he and Marlow had never got on: he withered with fear. Even Hopper beside him had moved on from Hawkins, and was noising in Reed's ear, 'Mar-low . . . look at him up there. His father now, he was a man, and his boy's all lardy-dar!'

Pethick was uncertain again when he looked at Riley, and noticed that whenever Hawkins said something that displeased Riley, his bushy eyebrows knit and met in one, while when he approved they unfurled and rose like wings. Wherever he looked in the room, now, he couldn't escape those brows, they hovered through the air like a dense double cloud of black moths. The scales fell from his eyes: Hawkins and Marlow were men of straw, Nigel Riley was the boss. That was good news—Riley usually nodded to him with a friendly look.

Pethick came to quickly and shivered—his own name. It sounded an odd name in Hawkins's mouth. He listened dully to the public account of how he had been sacked: it did not quite seem to be about him.

Hawkins stopped. Pethick realized, it was for him to speak now, if he wanted to. He felt pressures and leanings from Reed to that effect. He suddenly thought, what to say? His mind emptied. He got to his feet. Inquisitive faces hovered in the air like pale balloons. He thought, these buggers are all against me. He opened his mouth, and words came:

'So, I shall not keep you long. You know what Clyde is, he is rude, he push you around, he is not right in the head. Today he give me the sack for nothing, for nothing at all. Warboys took the plates from me, he didn't ask, he just took them. Then he came back, he said "Do them!" Just like that. I said, no, no, NO. Today, this day, I WILL NOT BE DONE

LIKE THAT. So Clyde comes, and gives me the sack. I ask now, what you do about it? I have worked here many years, always I pay my money on the dot.' He paused, his voice sounded too loud and brittle: he knew he was losing ground. 'Perhaps you will do nothing. I don't know. But I think—I think there should be more people here tonight. Many years I work here. Well, I hope the people who are here, they care about justice, they do something for me. All right! I sit down. Thank you.' He sat.

No one spoke. The platers looked at the stained floor, at the pagoda columns of stacked glasses, at the butcher's poster of prime cuts stuck in irony on the wall. Reed, beside Pethick, said with weak emphasis, 'Oh, well said, Mares! That told them.' Pethick didn't believe him; and then, in a hot wash of shame, he saw his mistake. He had clean forgotten to aim his speech at Riley. It was all up now: a jagged weight solidified inside him, it was the iron weight of his distrust and dislike of these men he depended on. It would break him open if he didn't get fresh air. He had to get out. He got up suddenly and cried, 'All right, I leave you to it. I have spoken, you know how it is. I wait outside, you speak free. Wally here can speak for me—*if he wants to.*' Before anyone said anything more, he almost ran down the gangway: he was a grown man, but this run was a stumbling shamble, his legs flung out awkwardly and jolted on the floor. The door banged loudly after him.

Reed called out, 'Well, are we just going to sit mum? I say we do something!'

But all was silence; till a chair-leg squeaked and grated on the verge of speech, then turned into a gruff murmur, 'I don't see there's much we can do.'

Reed jumped on Barrett, who had spoken. 'What the hell

do you mean by that?' But Barrett only looked at Reed through narrowed knowing eyes. 'Wally. . . . you know . . .'

'I don't know, tell me!' Reed cried, though he did know.

Barrett would say no more: he had wrung one piece of action from the union tonight, he was embarrassed to ask for more.

Reed felt a tug at his coat-tail, and looked round. In the dimming canteen, the enormous rough bloodshot face of Hopper smiled up at him like the reflection of a setting sun, and gasped in a choking whisper, 'Wally, it's not the same. He isn't one of us.' Around them, a few deep voices repeated calmly, gravely, 'It's not the same.'

Reed tried to catch the eye of Bridger Jack, a quiet plater who had several times straightened as if he wanted to speak, but then slumped again. But when he caught the wide blue eye, it rolled away immediately and wouldn't come back. 'Lias Trigg sat with his head down and serious, but showed by his rigidity that he did not see fit to take the issue up. Reed looked at the three union dignitaries, and they were not evasive. They looked back quizzically, slightly sympathetic, with seasoned shrewd-ironic eyes that knew the Pethick business was simply not on.

Reed felt an embarrassment in the audience. Then it struck him, they were not embarrassed about Pethick, they were embarrassed on his own behalf: he was making a fool of himself. This sapped him, but still he cried, 'I wish George Reynolds were here, he'd have given us something choice about the union today.' Reynolds deeply disapproved of his successor, but forbore to interfere, and stayed away from union meetings now. Barrett sang out, 'Yes—or old Eric Strachey!' Strachey, once an activist, had been a permanent absentee ever since he had been passed over for Shop

Steward—the platers feeling that under a Strachey regime it would be down-tools or go-slow all the time, and they would get no bonus at all. The men laughed loudly, the tensions relaxed, and it was clear to everyone that the Pethick question was dead.

'Well, brothers,' said Hawkins, 'I don't think this one is going to get off the ground.' The meeting passed on to other things, and became, even, sprightly. Reed got up, and left as noisily as he could.

17

Pethick was tired, and in an odd stunned condition, as if his mind had been dislocated. During the long walk home what had happened today, and what had happened many years before, got confused with the way his clothes chafed and weighed on him and his boots hung on his feet like a diver's, and with the acid ache in his muscles. By the time he turned the last corner, he only wanted to put all of it off.

The road changed direction just where they lived, so that their house was wedge-shaped, in each room the walls converged. Pethick let himself in, and with a few steps he was at the back, looking out of the window of the tapering scullery. Their garden was a triangle. It had been a triangle of concrete when they moved in, but he hacked that up, and turned the stinking yellow soil to grass, and now the little patch was green as a rich pasture.

As he stealthily unwound the kitchen tap and ran the fizzing water cold, he looked out on his family. His wife sat forward in a deck-chair, with her lips compressed and her head on one side, giving her verdict on several brightly-coloured drawings which Ewa, their daughter, had spread out on the grass. Ewa worked in a design agency, and was their pride. Pethick was moved as he watched her, with her face warm and animated, leaning back every so often to feel the weight of her brown hair. He made a drink of lime and salt, and went outside.

His daughter looked up, 'Did you put a little lime-juice with the salt, Dad?' He smiled, and absently disturbed the white sediment in his glass. His good-humoured face looked worn and fallen in, but they thought only that he was exhausted.

The tiny garden was a sun-trap, and he took off his jacket and shirt and lay down on the grass. He felt a curious lightness, as though the moment before the blow fell had been frozen, and the pleasant relaxed evening could go on as it was for ever. But they were alert to something he gave away. His wife frowned at him fiercely, her glasses being weak. 'What's happened, Mares?' When he tried to say what he usually said, 'Marjorie, it's been a good old day,' his voice gave out. Both his women were on the scent now, and there was nothing for it but to tell them right away. He sat up stoopingly, looking at his knees, almost embarrassed, like a man who had done something he shouldn't.

His wife snatched off her glasses, blinked often, and fired off indignant questions so quickly that he scarcely made out the words. His daughter got up and paraded the tiny garden: the drawings flew, her legs flickered and danced, her curled hair and flared skirt jerked and twirled. Her words came in firm snaps. 'Oh, they can't do that! Who can we see? There must be someone.' Soon she was planning: there was the union branch office to go to; the personnel manager at the works. There was Barry in the Time Study—their friendship had been quite fraught, but they were close, she could go to see him. Could he help?

Now that Pethick's wife and daughter took up the burden, it became for the moment more theirs than his. He lay on his back, easing his burning skin on the cool grass. He was quiet now, oddly calm, removed from himself. The midges circled as his daughter spun, and dapple crept across her and the garden. From next door came the continuous quiet scuffle and throb as the pigeons milled in their stacked coops.

They went in to tea: and in the darkening greyness of the pale sunless room, the queer light mood of the garden was lost beyond recall. Mrs Pethick was silent now, thinking of the future. Pethick sat quite still, except that like a clockwork man he continually, absently, poured tea into himself. There was a shiver about his eyes, his quietness was so fragile it tore Ewa in two. She sat listening to the soft feathery fall of sugar on the surface of the tea. The family's sadness filled the room and deepened; it gathered in Ewa's head like a numb weight of lead.

A huge tiredness descended on Pethick as though, for the last hour, it stood just at his back. When his women had not known his trouble, they had pulled him out of it, but their steady clear outrage and sympathy now brought it all back to him with increase: so that even as their feeling poured towards him, he sank alone into a deep shaft where they could hardly reach him.

18

In the evening the dissolved Plate Shop, fed and refreshed, reconvened in the Bag of Nails. Nutty Saville had a pint ready for 'Lias Trigg.

'Mild's good tonight, 'Lias! *Straight* from the drip-tray!'

'Oh, I do like a bit of spit!' 'Lias took a long draught, while Saville asked, 'What happened, 'Lias? Is it: all out, down tools! ?'

'What, before Hawkins gets out of the red?'

'You shouldn't say that, 'Lias! That's only your idea.'

'It's a good'n, though.' 'Lias lounged across the bar, sipping his drink and studying the telly which blazed away on a high shelf with the sound turned off.

'Nothing about Mackworth Crowley, then?'

'Not a lot.'

'I don't like that, 'Lias. That's very odd.'

'I'll tell you what, Nutty. The little chap come unstuck.'

'Who's that, then?'

'You know, Nutty, the little chap who copped it.'

'Oh, Pevvick. Didn't you do nothing then?'

'Nah.'

'That's a bit rough.'

'It is rough. Yeah. You know what we did do?'

'Bugger all, it sounds like.'

'Yeah, well, if we had your record of attendance, Nutty, I doubt we'd get as far as that. No, what we did do is, we go slow till Barrett gets his bonus.'

'What! Not his big ends and his little ends?'

'Yeah.'

'Bloody hell! That's rough on Pethick, though, 'Lias.'

'It *is* rough.'

'I wonder you didn't say anything. Point of order, you know, point of order, Mr Chairman.'

'Point of order. Yeah. Well, Nutty, I thought it was poor. But, you know, nothing would have come of it. And I thought, what's Pethick to me? He's not *local*, is he?'

Victor Watts joined in, 'Pethick not local ! That's good, 'Lias. That's very good. He comes from bloody Czechoslovarkia!'

They all laughed, then Saville asked, 'Anything on the accident, 'Lias?'

'Nah. It's not ours, is it?'

Watts said, 'There was nothing in the local paper, you know.'

'That's typical.'

'There was nothing. There was just a little bit on an inside page. Said there'd been an accident, chap was in hospital, he was all right.'

'That's Strudwick for you.'

'Steady on, 'Lias ! Do you think that was Strudwick?'

'*Course* it was Strudwick! He's got the local paper tied up. He's only to pick up the phone. They play golf together, don't they?' 'Lias picked up a chair by the leg, and lightly swung a golf stroke with it. 'Nutty, I'll get you a drink.' He leaned across the counter and bawled into the next bar, 'Here! Angel! Darling mine!' The barmaid, a handsome middle-aged woman in horn-rims, shouted back, 'I'm on my way, honey-bunch.'

While she served them, Trout the labourer came swerving and tottering to the bar. She called to him, 'A baby Guinness, my sugar?'

Trout nodded. He hardly said a word in the pub, he had no one to talk to though half the factory was there. Before the awed eyes of Trigg and Saville he poured the baby Guinness straight down his throat, stood a moment digesting, then banged the bottle down on the bar and shouted in a thick clogged voice, 'Get us a *Mirror*! I want a *Daily Mirror*!' On cue Trigg, Saville and all the platers round paused in what they were doing and made a business of hunting out a *Mirror* for Trout. There wasn't one. 'There's a local paper, Bert.' 'Will the *Evening Standard* do, Bert?'

Trout chose the *Evening Standard*. 'Right. Cover the board. Cover the board so I can't see a thing.'

Trigg and Victor Watts made a rigmarole of wedging the newspaper so it hung out over the dartboard. Trout stared round with eyes all blood, and shouted hoarsely, 'All right, any number on the board. Tell me a number, and I'll hit it.'

The platers suggested, 'Go for the bull, Bert.' 'Treble twenty, Bert.'

Trout considered. 'All right. I'll take the treble twenty.'

He stood looking at the board, swaying slowly and blinking his horny eyelids as though he had dust in his eyes: his face had gone serious, and old and lined. He crooked his over-long arm, and the frayed sleeve rode back from the scrawny yellow wrist. But still his whole body, including the dart-arm and the dart, swayed slowly forward, and back, and forward again. The platers watched: if he let go at the right moment in his sway, he could do great things. He caught himself, when he had gone so far back he nearly fell, then he swung forward again, his arm went down, the dart hurtled from his hand.

There was a crack like a gun-shot: he had missed the board completely. But in the face of this defeat, he only turned away from the dartboard absently, as though he had forgotten what he was doing. One of the platers at the bar got a whisky for him; he drank shorts and baby Guinnesses alternately. Trout took the drink and drained it, while the platers forgot him again.

Hawkins, Marlow and Riley, who had waited by the dartboard long-suffering but eagle-eyed, moved in and took possession. They needed a fourth, and Mrs Marlow, a known force, obliged. Mrs Marlow was a fine aquiline face, heavily made up, and a smart canary dress. While other wives sat round the walls of the pub gossiping subduedly and not taking their eyes off their husbands, Mrs Marlow chatted with the men. Now they played, and her lively strong feminine voice, laughing and chaffing, penetrated the pub.

The game was short. At a nearby table George Reynolds was finishing a hand of brag: the three men he was playing with glanced at his trick, then at their own, then at each other's, and three voices murmured, 'Yours, George.' With a slow sweep of his arm, Reynolds gathered the florins; then sat back, and in a strong grave voice that cleared a space for itself, he shouted out, "Lias!'—Trigg attended —'Did you happen to go to the union meeting?'

Platers near at hand muttered, 'Here we go!' 'Let rip, George.' 'This'll be bloody good.' Sly eyes turned to Hawkins at the dartboard: it was his throw, and he did not turn his head, but stood there motionless like a darts player turned to stone.

While Trigg told him what had happened, Reynolds nodded slowly. He noticed an apprentice counting out silver beside the juke-box, and caught his eye and held it till, after several tremors to the slot, the hand fell limp. Then Reynolds cleared his throat, and at the top of his voice, slowly, remarked, 'It's nothing to do with me. It's not my shop any more. But I'll say this—I don't know what the union's for, if it's not to help a good worker when he's down.' He looked selected platers confidently in the eye, and there was a rumble of wise agreement which came even from those who had been at the union meeting. But then there was a disturbance behind: Reynolds turned, and found at his elbow Hawkins, standing over him enraged.

'Is he getting at the union?' Hawkins shouted. 'He was a Shop Steward himself, now he's criticizing the union!'

Reynolds looked at him, surprised, for it was not pomposity, Hawkins truly was beside himself with indignation. Then Mrs Marlow joined in, with a strong clang. 'Yes, dammit George, if you disagreed, why didn't you go to the meeting?'

Reynolds's brows rose slowly. He disapproved too much

of women interfering in union affairs even to speak. He sat with dignity: he did not see her, he did not hear her, she was not there. Such a weight of non-existence told on Mrs Marlow, and she drew back — only to find that in the meantime the dartboard was usurped by Patrick Collier and the messenger-girl—she, no more than Mrs Marlow, was going to sit with wives. Then Mrs Marlow smiled indeed, like a knife being sweet.

But while Reynolds sat in victory and judgement a vibration ran through the pub. Everyone turned, to see a stout man of forty, with a red miserable face, who stood at the door with his coat awkwardly catching on his arm as he tried to get it off. It was Holmes, the electrician: by common consent, he was to blame for the crane-accident in the morning. Talk died.

Without once looking round, he walked to the bar. 'Edna, I'll have a pint.'

'Right you are, my treasure,' she said quietly. Holmes took the money from his pocket, but his fingers were clumsy as if bandaged.

The whole pub watched while he took a long swallow of his drink; then he called out, 'Well, Jack, how goes it?'

The plater nodded to him but hung his head, he was sheepish at being singled out.

Holmes said in a harsh, too-loud voice, 'I'll do the distributor on that car of yours. By God it needs it!'

'Thanks,' the plater muttered, embarrassed.

Holmes glanced round, then drank his way steadily through his pint. When he finished, he put the glass firmly down on the counter, and said generally, 'Well, I must be getting along. Evening all.'

He kept his face contained and set as he walked to the

door. He did not hurry. There was a drag or trip in his walk.

As soon as he had gone, everyone started talking. They wanted a change of mood, and presently Tony Wilmot, the singing plater, was called to perform. He was coy, his loose thatch modestly curtained his face, but he was coaxed and cajoled, and eventually his deep subterranean bass reverberated downwards as though it were singing upwards from the cellars of the pub:

'I went be-hind the coun-ter,

I thought I was not seen . . .'

He got going: he threw back his head, his full pint did not quiver in his raised hand, and with a zest of humour and self-humour he roared out for all the pub to hear

'The mar-garine turned pink and green

And all the eggs started 'atching.

Forty little chicks went cock-a-doodle-doo

In my old lavender trousers.'

Rising voices joined the chorus, but as they came in chaotic in the higher scales, Wilmot's beautiful voice only sang down octaves below the best of them, an unfathomable bass.

19

Late that night, Clyde's wife Jessie lay awake. Their bed-room was in the front of the house, and the cold green glow from the streetlamp seeped round the edges of the curtain, and crept in long fingers across the ceiling. She lay with only so much awareness as the room had light, but with no more chance of getting to sleep than a door kept ajar by a thin breeze has of closing itself.

She lay awake most nights. She had nothing to do all day, and when Clyde got back in the evening he was exhausted and wanted only to collapse. He wouldn't tell her about the things that wore him down. She felt he shut her out, and she knew it would be like this till they were dead. She had come to be jealous of the factory.

Today it was a lock-out. He came home in a foul mood and let his jacket drop on the tiles with a crash like a bundle of cymbals. At table he said nothing, and only piled her day's work of cooking into his mouth as though it made no odds to him what fine flavours decorated his fuel. For the rest of the evening he sat in front of the telly, not watching it and not speaking, with something displeased and peevish in his face as though he wanted something from her which she could not give, and which he had too much pride to ask for.

She was cold under the thin summer bedclothes, but hadn't the will to put anything warmer on the bed. Clyde lay beside her like a long hill. Then there was a catch in his breathing out, and the long voiced breath he made continued till it was a lung-emptying groan. He lay quite still. He could not stand much cover and a black arm was out on the bedclothes, while his large black head lay beside her aimed at the ceiling.

'Edward? Are you awake? What is it?'

But he only said, in the same low, voiced breathing like a groan, 'It's nothing, Jessie.' Presently there was a massive heaving and creaking, and a dragging wave shifted all the bedclothes as he turned on his side. His body moved slowly there, he couldn't get comfortable, and he rolled on his back again. Eventually he murmured, so she could hardly hear, 'A bad day, bad things . . . there was an accident . . . not my fault, but I always feel . . . do you know, I gave someone the sack.'

'Who was it?'

'Oh, who was it, blasted chap, foreigner, Pethick his name is.'

She hadn't heard of him. Almost all Clyde told her about the Plate Shop concerned the wisdom of George Reynolds and the looney antics of 'Lias Trigg. 'What did he do?'

'Oh, he asked for it, I had to do it.' He moved heavily, and all the bed and bedclothes rustled and disturbed with him. 'Trouble may come of it . . . Josh saw him talking to Hawkins, Shop Steward . . . I'll stand on what I did, I can't take him back.'

'I should hope so. And Edward—the General Manager, Stacey, he's behind you, isn't he?'

After a long pause, Clyde said in a low voice not like him

that seemed to draw the last curl of air from his lungs, 'My time's up, Jessie.'

She waited in the dark, fixed in attention, but his voice only got to her in snatches, almost smothered. 'Dawson . . . a good plater . . . be in good hands . . .'

She lay beside him helpless, he was at the bottom of himself. 'Edward, Edward, there'll be years yet. Years.'

She spoke to the darkness, and the darkness gathered and heaped towards her and took hold of her in a grip like a gentle wrench, 'Oh, there'll be years yet, there'll be donkey's years.' His voice had warmed and filled, though what he said meant nothing, he was simply voicing his concern that she shouldn't worry. The timbre of his voice took hold of her as his hand had done.

He lay back again, then for a long time they lay not asleep, but drifting in the surface vapours of sleep, while the night extended.

When Jessie came to again, hours had gone by. The streetlamp had gone out, but she was aware that a warm mountain loomed over her. Gradually she made him out, raised on one elbow, evidently he was studying her and had been studying her for a long time.

He was absorbed in just making out, in the first morning dimness, her lean clear-featured face, with its worn and kind lines. It was a fine face with delicate edges and corners. What of his face she could see was all suspended tender study of her.

In a soft growl he now asked, 'Jessie, are you awake?'

Surfacing towards his warm weight, keeping about her the lightest warm gauze of sleep, she murmured, 'I'm awake.'

20

The General Manager, Stacey, drove back from London in the small hours. He had finished the night drinking, and left town light-headed, and as he drove on lapped in a low dry warmth from the heater, with the radio softly crooning to him over the broad so-soft purr of the engine, and mesmerized by the battery of discreet green dials in front of him, he felt insulated, almost bodiless, like a rarified creature of the future cruising cushioned and cocooned within the hardened shell of an invulnerable projectile. His trouble sang to him incoherently, like shrieking in the distance, just as again the part of him that drove the car seemed a small ticking mechanism performing its functions at a far remove, like a computer hidden in the wall.

So shielded and cosseted, he only gradually woke to the fact that this automatic pilot inside him was driving slower and slower. They were running into a queue of cars with bright lights beyond them, and this he could not understand because he knew the present stretch of road was bare and straight for miles ahead. But apparently the lights indicated some form of road-works, and this idea seemed confirmed when he came in sight of a large machine, a generator or engine on four wheels, and men in tunics moving to and fro.

Something large swung through the air, they had a crane at work. A man bent down, working intently with a blow-torch—it was like an odd view of his own factory strung out along the highway. The queue of cars slowed until it inched forward, and through the haze it gradually came clear to Stacey that what he had thought was a generator was not that, it was a car-engine naked on the chassis, oddly dislocated, with the car-body torn off; and what he had thought was a long activity of roadworks, with trenches stretching away, was instead a terrible accident. As he crawled forward he was carried beyond preoccupation into dazzling shock, and by the end was moved to tears by the length of this crash. Perhaps it was only that he was half-drunk, tired, and affected by the discoveries of the day, but he drove on till it seemed there would be no end to the crushed shapes of steel, horribly flowered and opened. Policemen and men in overalls moved so busily among them in red lights, in brilliant flood-lights, in flashing sparking amber lights. Then a crumpled van with its body set all on the slant slowly raised its front part in the air like a wounded creature. So he realized, it was an old accident, the terrible crashing and shrieking that had gone on and on, that was still dawning in his mind, had all happened hours before, all the ambulances were gone, and the road at last half-cleared to let traffic through: he was looking into a past of destruction which he had not known existed when it happened. Then all at once truly it was past, and like the lights of a huge grandstand all suddenly switched off at once, he was thrust into such pitch-blackness as he had not known. He drove on mechanically but slowly as though in the crash half of him was scooped away.

All he did to steady himself as he drove was to rest his hand on the large folder he had beside him on the front seat, the two words on its cover clear in his mind however dark it got. It had been the day of days, though no one at home knew anything of it yet.

He was nearly back. Now he could just see the city—a long jagged edge on the horizon like a strip of torn iron, against a low rusty panel of light.

Within the city, behind long walls and locked gates, in a wide plain with no one in sight, row after row of marshalled machines slowly came clear. In a tall building a cold glassy twilight crept through slats into an endlessness of empty offices. In the thick darkness of the Plate Shop a brown glimmer just gathered to a small face, fixed, rapturous, faint as a coil of smoke, the pale bright face of Marilyn Monroe.

Second Day

116

21

When Ewa Pethick crested the hill, the entire city lay below her in an enormous bowl, sunlit, silent. The brown estates, green parks and grey factories were glistening and sharp-edged to the horizon, as if the fresh breeze that met her were a clear stream that had washed the city all night. On the far rim a long blue works stood guard: the metal stems of its chimneys looked delicate and brittle as if they were made of glass.

The city was a great still wheel, waiting to turn: and all so bright and keen that her hopes couldn't not gather. She plunged full-pelt down an empty road. Desperate times, desperate measures.

In a broad grassy estate she propped her bike on a low tile wall dotted along the top with tiny plants that looked made of green rubber. The house had a wide drive to some large concrete space behind it, and a cat's cradle of concrete walks in its tiny front garden.

The frosted glass darkened and a lean woman opened the door.

'Mrs Spurrier. I know it's not a good time, I'm very sorry. I wanted to see Barry.'

The amazed woman collected herself with difficulty, and

117

said over her shoulder, 'It's not the post. Barr-ee!' She elongated and flattened against the wall, so Ewa could come in.

Ewa entered, to find Barry Spurrier the time-studier sitting in state over the dereliction of a breakfast-table such as the Pethicks never contrived, bobbing with orange-peels, ribboned with bacon-rind, cluttered with jams and marmalades and a litter of pills, white, primrose, fawn and peaty, in which Barry's mother believed. Jacketless and untied, Barry sat at his ease over the exhausted banquet, while his father, a bald, burly, red man, proprietor of several lorries, sat on the stove, warming his seat as he read the paper. He looked up and smiled at Ewa. His bright brown eyes didn't know who she was, didn't care, and approved. But Barry's mother was a standing narrowness beside her.

Barry stood up, embarrassed and alarmed, and also glad to see her.

'What's happened, Ewa?'

She started to explain. Barry's father saw that something serious and bad had happened, and sat waiting, sympathetic and inquisitive, to hear what it was. He was drawn off by Barry's mother into the living-room, from where, through the serving-hatch, her loud whisper rose. 'What a time to call! A funny girl. Oh dear.'

As Ewa told Barry what had happened, the bright morning went cold and dead for her, and her alert shoulders folded in. She only told him the facts, but they pulled her back and trapped her again in the bad night the Pethicks had had.

Barry was full of indignation, the platers' union were capable of anything—but what could be done now? After first exclamations he sat moving the vitamin-pills like counters, disturbed by doubts that he worked to hide. His father came back into the kitchen, and stood near the door making a large red cloud of generosity in the corner of Ewa's eye. Through the serving-hatch the hectic panting of punched cushions stopped.

Barry could only say, over and over, 'Don't worry, Ewa. We'll set this to rights.' But he didn't sound confident. Ewa stood awkwardly, uncertain now, and not sure how best to retreat.

They went outside, Barry's car was next to the house. They had been in and out of each other's lives for a year or more, there were always tensions between them—his work, especially, had been the barrier. But now all provocation fell away. Barry shared Ewa's burden, and they came to a curious pause, unguarded, in which Ewa felt weak, and the tight knot in her melted. Barry saw this, but couldn't adjust: he was late, late, there was time to be studied. He said quickly, 'Don't worry, Ewa. We'll get things moving.' He started his car, and drove off with purpose.

Ewa, left, was glad, and sorry, and not certain what it was that was not right. She wheeled her bike round with her father's sad, ironic pucker gathering in her face.

'This is a very bad thing,' Barry's father said. He had come outside and stood beside her on the pavement commiserating. He said little, he only stood there, quietly glowing with a deep sympathizing kindliness.

'Shall I run you into town?' he asked. He went round the back of the house, and presently, from the hidden cemented yard where he tinkered in the evenings, a large truck, of the capacity of his sympathy, emerged in rumbling thunder. He lightly heaved Ewa's bike into the back, helped her clamber into the quaking cab, and they started.

22

When he reached the factory, Barry did not go straight away to Forbes. Instead he went down a low echoing tunnel, between two steel doors jammed against the walls with hunks of iron, and out into the enormous hall of the Plate Shop, where the platers in blue overalls and leather aprons walked and chatted in no great hurry, and where a labourer, bent down like an ox, heaved past him tugging a low trolley stacked high with plate: the axles shrieked. He walked among trees of gadgetry, beneath high belts revolving and slapping in mid-air; the fire from the forge blew like breath from a loose mouth into the large tin chimney.

Barry came at last to a part of the shop where the roof-structure changed, where the walls were painted cream, and where everything was quieter, cleaner and lighter. In this bright area the fitters assembled the new machines. Barry walked briskly on, and let the plater he wanted to see call after him, 'Hey, Barry! Wup there, Mr Spurrier! No hard feelings, old chap, but you left the stabilizer off of this card.'

'The stabilizer? What are you on about?'

The moment Barry paused, a stringy fair-complexioned man, with shy, sly, amused blue eyes, heaved himself off a supporting girder, laid his long stomach half across an engine, and, propping up his front end on his elbows, started poking and stabbing at his job-card with a biro. He plunged into a tangle of sums. It was early and sunny; the man's mouth kept smiling at the corners; and Barry was almost hypnotized by the large supple hand that lightly flicked over the white card in a dance of hieroglyphs. The biro was everywhere at once; the figures would not stay still; and indeed, every time Barry looked, there seemed to be something different about them. Eventually he said,

'Stop a minute, Bridger. What's that fifty doing there?'

'The fifty? Oh, Mr Spurrier, don't you know what that is?' And he went on, till Barry put his hand on the card, and simply gazed at the fifty, rapt. Then Bridger, who was at first much surprised, caught Barry's perplexity by invisible infection, and just gazed with him at the fifty, his comrade in wonder—till light suddenly dawned, he struck himself on the forehead and cried, 'Oh, I could kick myself!' But instead of kicking himself he crossed out the fifty, he obliterated it utterly, and turned to Barry, radiant. And at that point Barry left everything in suspense, and inquired, 'Bridger, I heard they had a meeting last night, about Pethick and that.'

'Mr Spurrier, I was there.'

'Oh?'

As coming to more serious matters, Bridger half-stood, and leaning askew and sag-shouldered off one straight arm, proceeded, 'You know, Barry, there was a lot of palaver, but the point is, those silly buggers wouldn't do a blind thing for that poor little bleeder. But then, old Wally, he gets a bee in his bonnet, he blew his top. I said to myself at the time, "Oh by Christ!" I said, "That's not the way to win your case, old chap!" And I damn near told him so to his face—but I thought better of it. But then you know, old Wally, he's no speaker. Well, then dear old good old Harry Hawkins (my old friend) he gets on his hind legs, and shakes a bit, and says, "Begging your pardon, bruvvers, I hate to say this, but is there something to be said for Pevvick's case? Do you think?" And all their heads go down, and they hold their heads in their hands like puddings. Then Hawkins says, "Bruvvers, he has a grievance, I can't deny, but bruvvers—he ain't English. He ain't one of us!" Then all the brothers, their heads come up, they throw up their hands, "Oh Gawd strufe!" they say, "Not English, not one of us!" I'd half a mind to say right out, "He's bloody Union, isn't he? Isn't that what sodding counts?" But what difference would that have made? I'll tell you, none. Then blasted old—the man, 'Lias Trigg, he sits stirring his stumps for five minutes, then he gets up and says, "Yes, brothers, old bully-beef jolly old fat-faced Edgar Warboys was telling me all about it, Pethick don't have a leg to stand on, and dear old Clyde, he done the right thing for once." Then Jimmy Marlow chips in, "Little ruddy bleeders," he says, "Send 'em back home! " Then they all shake their heads, no go, not a hope, no chance, that's that. And that was that. And Hawkins was standing up there all smarmy and cocky with it, why I damn near stood up there and then and told him right out to his face what I thought of him, only I left him to it, it was a bloody farce, Mr Spurrier, the whole bang shoot.'

Now he had the first-hand and guaranteed account he wanted, Barry could proceed. He insinuated into Bridger's card a modest discretional allowance of an hour, and set off to see what engines of repair and justice a small touch in the right place could set in motion.

*

When Barry got to the Time Study office, Forbes was detailing the orders of the day, and giving Bert Cherry no rest. Cherry stood sullen before him, puffing out sweet smoke like a steam-engine, as if he wanted to fumigate Forbes.

When Forbes returned to his office, Barry waited a moment, then tapped on his door.

'Come in,' said the pleasant-timbred voice.

Barry approved of Forbes's office, which was neat and austere. All it had in it were three filing cabinets in a row, charts hung on the walls wherever it was easiest to see them, and papers and trade-journals arranged in tidy piles. Forbes's desk was old, but differed from other desks in being a robust and solid piece of timber. His chair likewise, which did not swivel or rock or go on castors, and had no cushions. All this spoke to Barry of Forbes's absorption in his work: he had what he needed and wanted no perks. Forbes had been studying the wide pages of the Control Book, where the performances of all the platers were averaged and percentaged out, in a tiny grid of ruled red lines, so as to show no change in as many ways as science could contrive. But at once Forbes disengaged from that, and with fresh alertness attended to Barry. Barry admired Forbes—Forbes was his idea of a good manager—but he was suddenly ill-at-ease as he looked at the pale tight-skinned piercing face and the severe waiting eyes.

'Mr Forbes, I wondered if you'd heard yet what happened about Pethick?'

At once the Pethick case, and the scheme for disposing of Clyde, swung into Forbes's sights. 'No, I hadn't.'

'They wouldn't do a thing for Pethick.'

'Tell me more, Barry.'

Barry told him all. Forbes's direct eyes took in the news, and at the end he said gravely, 'I'm very sorry.'

Barry waited. Forbes waited.

'I wondered, Mr Forbes. What do you think the next step is?'

Forbes was surprised, 'The next step, Barry?'

'I suppose you'll be seeing Strudwick. I just wondered what the best way is, to see justice is done.'

There was a quick flicker across Forbes's face, like a change of slide in a projector. 'Oh, but Barry, I'm not sure what we can do about that now.'

A drop of freezing water had touched on Barry's neck: Forbes's decency was an article of faith.

'I only wondered, Mr Forbes, what is the best way, now, to do the right thing by Pethick.'

Forbes studied Barry with a kind of tight sympathy. 'Well, Barry, Pethick is a very good driller—he'll get work anywhere he wants. There's no question about it. And, damn it all, do you think he'd want to come back here, after what they've done to him?'

Barry was tense and pale: he had found Forbes out, he wasn't decent. 'Oh yes of course, Mr Forbes, I only meant, if Pethick was *wrongly* sacked . . .'

'Oh well, but Barry, the union won't say that, you say. And I think we can bet Clyde won't say it . . .' He gazed at Barry, as if he had just realized that Barry might need glasses.

Barry said quietly, 'Ah, I see, Mr Forbes, you think that what we ought to do about this, to settle the matter, would really be to drop Pethick because the union won't back him.'

But Forbes would not go so far. He gave Barry a sharp cold drill of a look, to make it clear, in subtle abundance, that he was pushing too hard. But Barry didn't respond: it seemed that an extraordinary obtuseness had thickened his head. Forbes sat back in his chair, and took in the signs that Barry was there to stay. A silence extended, and the two men were still, like fixtures in the austere still office.

Forbes turned the situation round in his mind. Then he thought, Why not? Everything had been organized to dispose of Clyde; it was a long shot now, and yet . . . He looked hard at Barry, then said decisively, 'Leave it with me, Barry. I'll talk to Strudwick.'

Barry looked at him, surprised and confused. Forbes repeated, in a clipped voice that made a full stop to the interview, 'Leave it with me, Barry.' Coldly dropping Barry en route, he headed back through the Time Study office, his coat-tails flying after him. His smile and nod rocked towards the time-studiers after he had left, while Pethick's fortunes travelled with him.

23

Forbes tapped, with technical deference and no respect within, on Strudwick's door.

'Come in,' a broad voice bawled.

Forbes opened the door, to find Strudwick loudly busy on the phone. He slipped into a spacious, dazzling office, where the new strip-lighting gleamed with cold stickiness in the newly-painted walls. With the air-conditioning that Strudwick had installed, it was like stepping into a breezy fridge. But though it struck so cold that Forbes huddled his jacket round him, Strudwick had his jacket off, his neck open, his sleeves rolled up. He was always so, partly to show that he was still the working man, and partly as an aid to keeping wide awake. His shirt was white as frost, his suit-trousers were newly pressed, his jacket hung dapper on a hanger behind the door: he was as clean and spruce as Forbes himself (though Forbes tended to navy, Strudwick to light, sheeny, aluminiumish cloth). Strudwick interrupted himself on the phone to say over his shoulder in his brusque Yorkshire, 'Ray? You're well? Take a pew.'

The pew was as new as the paintwork, the strip-lighting, and the air-conditioning, for when Strudwick modernized a factory, he made sure he started at home. This pew swivelled on a rigid chrome tripod, it was high-backed and thick-armed in black plastic leather. It was all soft flop and give as Forbes let himself into it, but as his weight settled it breathed out, went firm, and snugly adjusted to his hams.

Forbes leaned back, and drily took in Strudwick. The man was fat, athletic and gingery: his plump forearms had large orange freckles and were fluffy with marmalade fur; ginger tufts of moustache and eyebrow curled and bristled about his tiny grey eyes and small turned-up nose. These gingery curlings made his face fierce in repose, and, wide-awake over the negotiating table, ferocious: and what stood behind the face was practical, single-minded and impetuous. Though he was brisk and exact like Forbes, Forbes loathed him. He always knew too much what he wanted, and went straight at it regardless of impediments. As to getting what he wanted, he almost had it, for as Works Manager he was only two rungs below director. True, those two rungs meant four moves: he would become General Manager of a small firm, then General Manager of a big firm, then Managing Director of a small firm, and so at last to Managing Director of a giant. But, what! for a heavily-built man he had small quick feet, deft nimble trotters, and he was only in his forties: he would make Director well before fifty. He was a bird of passage, and was constantly at odds with Forbes, whose ambition was to stay with one firm, overhaul it steadily and thoroughly, and grow with it as it steadily grew. But Forbes felt his diplomacy was equal to Strudwick's fire; and the factory would never be Strudwick's, in the way that it was his.

Strudwick, on the telephone, was winding up, 'You do all that— p.d.q., mind, no sitting around on your back-side. And Cynthia, get the file on Davis Engineering, I want it right away. All right? Right.' He slammed down the phone, twizzled round like a whirligig on his swivel, then stamped his feet on the floor so he stopped dead, staring at Forbes. 'Ray! Well?'

'Nothing from Crowley?' Forbes inquired, but casually. He was engrossed in the long fight with Clyde, and even if news had come, he almost wanted not to know it, till he had settled Clyde's hash.

'Not yet,' Strudwick said, so briskly and cheerfully that Forbes wondered whether he did have news. But he decided that Strudwick simply felt on top of the world, as he usually did, and was not prepared to stop feeling like that unless made to by force. And while Strudwick's face was uncertain, his body leaned back of itself, his arms and legs stretched wide, and his toes flexed with pleasure.

Coming to the office, Forbes had wondered whether he should creep up on his subject with cunning, or whether, in dealing with Strudwick, he should do what Strudwick did, and go straight at it like a bull at a gate. One glance at the blunt face before him, so ready to chafe, reminded him that with Strudwick nothing succeeded like manly directness, and he inwardly squared his shoulders, and aimed himself at his gate.

'Carl,' he said, 'I'm at the end of my tether. Something's got to be done about Clyde, and it's got to be done soon. I can't go on running this new scheme, trying to get it going, when every move I make is blocked, hindered, mucked up — when I'm held up at every turn by his sheer obstinate bloody-minded cussedness.'

Strudwick's eyes shrank in shrewdness. 'What's he done now?'

'He's sacked Pethick out of hand.'

'Who's Pethick when he's at home?'

'Pethick? You know Pethick, Carl. The little Czech, works the Pillar Drill. Oh I'm really surprised you don't know about him.'

'Wait a bit, I do—little runty chap, weak in the head. Go on.'

'He's as good a driller as we've got,' Forbes said reproachfully, 'You ask any fitter in the shop.'

'Well, well?'

'We can't afford to lose him like that. I want him back, and to be honest with you, Carl, if Clyde won't have it, I think Clyde should go. Frankly, Carl, it's got to that point with me, where if it were a choice between letting Clyde go, and letting a skilled craftsman be kicked off the shop floor, I'd let Clyde go just like that.'

Forbes had put his cards on the table with a flourish that had Strudwick sitting back and blinking. After a moment he sat forward, snatched up the phone, and shouted, 'Cynthia, got those files? Good. Put 'em away, I shan't need them now. I want my memoranda on Edward Clyde—and Cynthia, I want them now.' Then he sat back and said shortly, 'Tell me what happened.'

Forbes told him. He trod lightly on Warboys's faults, and Strudwick himself seemed more than ready to back Warboys in every step he took, and to run down Clyde.

When Forbes finished, Strudwick sat forward, frowning, with arms firmly clasped. Forbes saw that he was now engaged in the quick thinking that he was famous for. Forbes hardly breathed: this moment was crucial.

Strudwick glanced up, 'What's the union say?'

'The union? Oh, I think there's a meeting in the offing.' Strudwick was Yorkshire and shrewd and not to be had, 'They're not too interested, eh?'

Forbes was non-committal.

Strudwick, in the event, was genuinely indignant, 'Ee, the buggers!'

Forbes was uncertain what to say. He had meant to conjure up a distant clink of tools downed. But Strudwick only sat there, gazing at his blotter, his stout face sharpened and intent. Then, abruptly, Strudwick looked up, and looked Forbes frankly in the eye, 'Of course, you're perfectly right, Ray. Clyde will have to go.'

It came so quick and easy, Forbes's eyes opened like doors. He was so used to thinking of Clyde as a permanency, as a tangle of thorn clenched into the soil with roots like iron hawsers, as an obstacle it would take dynamite to remove. It shook him, to discover that Clyde could be tipped so easily.

There was a faint pat on the door. It opened slowly, and a stooping girl with a pale, ill face and watery eyes came nervously in with a folder.

'Cynthia! Good girl! You can take it back, we've dealt with that. Get some tea for Mr Forbes and myself. P.d.q.'

This, coming now, surprised Forbes, though normally he enjoyed the little snacks and drinks for which Strudwick was always finding pretexts whenever Forbes, or anyone else, came to see him.

Strudwick picked up a prospectus and tapped his desk quickly with it. He seemed busy trying to look as though he had nothing on his mind; and Forbes, at that point, began to suspect him.

Casually, half in abstraction, Strudwick seemed to discover himself in the distance remarking, 'Tell me, Ray, if we do get rid of Clyde—did you have any thought, as to who we might put in his place?'

Forbes tautened, and as in innocent curiosity inquired,

'Have you, Carl?' The succession was everything.

Strudwick stretched himself, 'Oh, there's no question about it, Ray—'

He paused. But Forbes, though he had no doubt that the next foreman should be Dawson, was not going to hand over his nominee too soon. He did, though, need to know Strudwick's. He opened his mouth as if to speak, but then didn't say anything—a device which he had always found made Strudwick start talking at once: which Strudwick did. With sudden energy he said,

'Tell me, Ray—what do you say to—you've mentioned the name yourself—to Warboys?'

'Warboys?!'

Strudwick sang out in admiration, like a man inspired, 'He's the chap! He's the man to get this place going again!'

Forbes was so confounded he could hardly speak. But, caution, he allowed, 'Warboys is a good charge-hand, Carl, I'll grant you. But Carl—has he got there yet?'

He hesitated doubt, but Strudwick had no great gift of doubt. 'Ray, he has!' Strudwick became confidential. 'Ray, I've had my eye on that man. I'll tell you, he's not a patient man. He's not. He calls a spade a spade. But he's got his head screwed on. He knows what's what. He doesn't beat about the bush. He's a man who sizes a thing up, and then he damn well gets it done!' Strudwick had been steadily heating, and his Yorkshire broadening, as he spoke, and now he got up and walked about the office. He no longer could sit still, and his strong baritone burst out 'Ray, Ray, you saw him lift the crane off that poor lad. Ee, Ray, the shoulders that man's got! It warms my heart to see him, he's champion, he'll put things to rights, he's the man we want!' He stared full at Forbes, evidently thinking that so he could coerce Forbes's agreement.

But Forbes sat downcast. From what Strudwick said, Forbes gathered that he was backing Warboys because he had decided that Warboys was like himself. Forbes almost laughed, for even Clyde was more like Strudwick than Warboys was. That of course was why Strudwick and Clyde could not get on. But oh, to reach the end of the long, difficult path, and to find there, Warboys: Forbes felt that life was not just.

Strudwick gazed shiningly at Forbes. He saw that Forbes wouldn't kindle, so he firmly added, 'He's a responsible man, Ray. He's very responsible.'

Forbes conceded, 'I'll allow that he's quick, very quick.' Warboys's rapid scrappy work, that just, by a hair's breadth, passed muster, was a known quantity in the shop.

'He's fast !' Strudwick exclaimed with relish.

Forbes, who had after all his own sense of humour, reflected, 'He certainly gets through as much work as anyone. You don't think—Carl—that he's—too good to take off the shop-floor?'

Strudwick only burst out laughing like a barbaric god of thunder. 'Oh, Ray, what argument is that? Come on, man, admit it. You're with me really, I can see you are. We'll call Stacey right away.' Strudwick picked up the phone, dialled for the General Manager, and shouted, 'Mr Stacey, Strudwick here. Have you a minute? Something very important. We'll be over right away.'

Forbes realized aghast that Strudwick was now in the process of striking while the iron was hot, which also he was famous for doing. And Strudwick banged down the phone, came round his desk like a boxer from his corner, and somehow shot into his jacket. He gave Forbes a brisk accelerating knock on the shoulder, swung the door open, and moved at speed through the offices, banging the doors back on their hinges so that Forbes had to hop and skip to avoid being caught on the rebound.

In the office of serene Mrs Bagnold, head of Sales, they swept past flustered Cynthia, hurrying the other way with a tin tray of clinking, chipping cups.

'No time for that,' Strudwick called from the next office. Cynthia was caught in the eddies, she spun round, the tray tipped, she tripped, and all the crockery hurled shattering on the floor. Into the amazed face of Mrs Bagnold Cynthia burst into tears, not briefly, but as if a dam of grief were breached at last.

Strudwick was swinging across the factory yard. Forbes hurried after, feeling the heat after Strudwick's office, but absorbed in his determination to keep Warboys out. When he looked up, the sight of the wide empty gate of the factory for some reason puckered and stirred a dim sediment on the floor of his memory, and he remarked:

'What should we do about Pethick?'

'Pethick? Oh, Pethick—we'll see about that with Stacey—'

They crossed the courtyard, and attacked the General Offices like a tornado. Cashiers flew, papers circled, secretaries merged into the wall, as Strudwick bowled through office on office to the great office up many stairs that commanded the factory. No power in the works was higher than Stacey. If Ewa could know, she would be glad that her father's case, against the odds, and with much else picked up by the way, was making speed at last with the impetus of a cannon-ball to the top.

24

Something flaccid and dark stretched in a lean sprawl across the large armchair in the hot office. The warm sunlight flowed in, but the windows were closed, and the dark panelled room slowly burned. The air was thick with specks and motes of dust that slowly, incessantly, descended through the streaming sun. The dust felt as if it had got into his parched eyes: it hurt to have them open, but he couldn't doze if he closed them. Nor could he shake off the warm stale drowse that had crept along his limbs and threaded his body. He couldn't wake, he couldn't sleep. He couldn't sit, he couldn't lie. He smoked desultorily.

Abruptly there was violent perturbation in the shining motes, they bellied round like thick smoke, and the door flew open as if it had been hit by a truck. Through the haze appeared the round pink face of Strudwick, and, behind, the pale bespectacled face of Forbes. The noise of the door, as it hit a bookshelf, brought Strudwick to his senses, and the two men hesitated on the threshold, blinking and peering into the haze.

With the dust was mixed the smoke of Stacey's cigarettes. Forbes and Strudwick waded through the dense, glowing atmosphere and sat down. But though they were just across the table from Stacey, it was still hard to see him, for the smoke hung round him in sunshot silvery skeins that lazily shifted, coiled, languorously drew out and turned over. Forbes could just see the dull black of Stacey's eyes, looking straight at him with a heavy set gaze that disconcerted him steadily more, the more he made it out.

The gaze switched to Strudwick, a moment after he started speaking. 'It's about the Foreman of the Plate Shop, Mr Stacey—Clyde. Forbes here is fed up. He's at the end of his tether, poor chap, and frankly I don't blame him. We can't go on as we are. Something's got to be done, and done soon.'

The torpedo was shot off, and disappeared in smoky silence. It seemed Stacey never heard what was said to him, but let the words fall to the ground, and only then stooped down, picked them up carelessly, and forced a tired reply. He quietly drawled, 'Edward Clyde . . . he's been here since the war.'

Strudwick nodded vigorously, and fired again with his usual boom. 'He has! Time was, when you couldn't have found a better Foreman on this side of England! But times change, and maybe he's been here a sight too long by now, by God.'

Again they waited, as though the words had to land on a distant target.

'It may be,' Stacey murmured, with a deep shrug. 'What's he done?'

'Ray can say best.' The heavy eyes swung back to Forbes, who related what had happened as best he could. He jumped each time Strudwick chipped in, deafeningly, in support of Warboys. 'He helps his friends, does Warboys!' 'He took the plates back himself!' 'He said he'd go to the Foreman, and so he had to. Quite right too.' But Stacey seemed not to notice the interruptions.

Forbes concluded. Then, quite at a tangent, Stacey asked Strudwick, 'What did you say the job was? Offside Guards? Hm. Strachey, eh?'

Forbes and Strudwick glanced at each other: they were back to square one, Stacey was worse even than usual. And he had once been an executive whose energy and purpose could never slow down or falter. Then, one year, he had simply stopped. All his taut muscles had relaxed of themselves, and gone slack. He himself seemed no more to know where the energy had gone, than Strudwick or Forbes knew where the electricity came from that tingled at their fingers' ends. With an instinct of health, they had averted their eyes from the run-down; and Stacey still went through the motions, with his experience he couldn't not do so. But neither Forbes nor Strudwick could help seeing, with annoyance, that he came ever later in the morning, and left ever earlier in the afternoon; that he lost his thread when they spoke to him; that he didn't change his clothes; that his blotter was covered with loose wavy spreads of tracery, where theirs had taut geometry, whether it was the concentric circles of Strudwick, or the neat squares of Forbes. Through a hundred tokens Stacey betrayed his standstill, and the sense of it percolated downwards so that there was perhaps no-one in the works who did not know that he had gone to seed, just as, it seemed, there was no-one who did not know that his marriage was slowly splitting on the rocks; that his affair with his fancy lady in the Dundee Road made slow progress; even, that his daughter was growing up strange, and that he saw, cared, and did nothing about it. And yet, leanly, darkly, stalking through the work-shops, he still had presence: that he did keep up. A tall man, untroubled by his height, he cut a figure in his sharp-edged grey-black suits, with his lean nose projecting downwards in fastidious disapproval, and his eyes momentarily observant through preoccupation, as he walked through the works with the ease of possession.

In his presence Forbes and Stacey were insecure, they wanted not to be where he was. Presently Stacey said:

'How long did you say Clyde had been with us?'

'Forty years,' Strudwick snapped impatiently; Forbes prayed that he would lose his temper completely.

'Forty years,' Stacey murmured over, with a weary wonder. Then, as if he had just woken, he sat forward, and at the same moment a cloud outside hid the sun, and all the light haze surrounding Stacey disappeared. Both Forbes and Strudwick saw in desolate clarity the long face, with its hard, shiny, roughened skin, with a red play of vein near the surface; the heavy eyes, with yellowing and veined whites; the black hair with lines of silver in it, carelessly groomed; and the soiled crumpled corner of shirt-collar that, in a General Manager, made both the under-managers wince. It was a bleak face, airless.

'I want to be sure I've got this right. You tell me that Clyde sacked Pethick because when Pethick got his job back—the job he'd been given—because when he was able to do it, and Clyde told him to do it, he refused to do it. Right?'

Strudwick came in quickly. 'It isn't only this, of course. There have been, oh, so many things.' Strudwick prepared to list them, but Stacey stopped him with his hand. Strudwick sat back, and said emphatically:

'He's got to go.'

Stacey looked dwellingly at Forbes, who with all his urgency said, 'He's got to go.'

While Stacey looked at them, the sun came out again, and he sank back relaxing into the radiant cloud. With a heavy fall of breath he said, 'Oh well then, of course, if he's got to go, he's got to go.' And then he laughed. And then there was another silence. Forbes and Strudwick fidgeted: this was not the way it should be done.

After a pause of gravity, Strudwick preened his suit. 'Oh, by the way—' a thought had struck him— 'I had turned over in my mind the question, who'd be a good man to put in Clyde's place.'

'Clyde's place?' Stacey murmured, gradually surfacing. An expiring tired tenderness in his voice suggested to Forbes that he had been momentarily away on the high seas, yachting with his mistress, Mrs Cook. But Forbes had no yacht, no spare time, and no mistress. He quietly said, fading in his voice so it should seem the mere continuation of Strudwick's thought,

'Yes, there is this man in the Plate Shop, Dawson. He's been a charge-hand for some years now. He's very good, very skilled, he's a very good plater. And he's the only man there that all the others look up to.'

Strudwick was thrust into a red trance; but came out of it quickly. 'Ray, Ray!' he cried, as though recalling to the point a forgetful and wandering Forbes, 'Dawson's out!'

'Out, Carl? Oh, but surely— Why, Dawson's far and away the best plater in the shop, he's much the most skilled man there. Who is there in the shop, who does better work?' Forbes stared at Strudwick, braving him. Yet Strudwick merely brushed smooth a wrinkle in his trousers. Forbes wondered quickly, had he made a slip?

'Come on, Ray,' Strudwick said. 'That's just the point. We discussed it, don't you remember? Dawson's too good a plater to take off the floor, his work is much too good. He'd be wasted in admin.'

'Too good? What argument is that?' Forbes asked, with calm contempt, and raging inward self-reproach. To gain time, he changed the subject, 'Oh, before we forget, should we just sort out what we do about Pethick? Shall we keep him on?'

'Keep him on?' Strudwick exclaimed hotly, ready to oppose Forbes on principle, whatever the topic.

Just then, however, there was a large jostling and dancing of the motes round Stacey, and he slowly uncoiled, vertical and dark, over them. He stalked to the window, and gazed out over the factory and townscape. He murmured something to himself, and they thought he was wool-gathering, but presently he looked round and said clearly, 'I'm glad you two came today. I had to see you, something has come up that affects all this.'

At the new note in his voice, Forbes and Strudwick instantly said to themselves, 'He's heard from Crowley.' But if Stacey did now know what was to happen in the future of all of them, he did not immediately say. And it struck Forbes that Stacey was nervous. To his surprise, his mind reverted to the last works dinner: when Stacey had not only an audience to contend with, but a lot of barracking from the platers at the back. He had presence, but not a loud voice. The audience strained to listen, he strained to be heard, the atmosphere was taut, nervous and difficult. The clapping and laughs came in to oblige, but they came each time a moment too late. In that situation Stacey gazed at a distant balloon on the far side of the hall, and his eyes nervously, quickly, flickered over his listeners and then returned again to the balloon. So, now, his eyes kept making for the window; and indeed, though he had something to say, he had also something to see, for one of his large projects had matured this morning. Forbes and Stacey went to stand on either side of him at the large window, and there, in his fitful, tardy, circling way, Stacey talked, and stopped, and talked again, and the other two heard and took in what he said, while the eyes of all three did not move from the large rectangle of glass and the something momentous that it showed.

25

They saw, in these accelerating times, a summer townscape: sunlight falling like fresh water on the tight country; clear light sparkling in the clanking lengths of chain that dragged away along the shining rails; while on the distant chalk line of motorway, the continuous purr of cars slid by as lightly as, oh as gaily coloured as (red, yellow, green) a paper chain.

Beyond the factory was a sunlit tower block, all its iron and concrete tonnage turned to lightness, lift and spring. To make it weightless, the architect had set back its trunk into the shadows, and had run round it an arcade of spindles so the granite tower poised sprightly on tip-toe. The plate glass hinted at ferned and trellised offices: almost like birdsong, there, the quick skittish patter of keys and ripple of chatter. These summery diamond towers receded across the city, they sprang up like young Atlases to share their burden easily, the high spotless dome-roof of the general workshop, where invisible machinery overhead caught the sun to make creeping stars in the day sky.

The factory itself was spread out like a garden. Its carpark was gay as a flower-bed, the coloured cars all washed and glowing. The apprentices' choppers glittered chrome all over, with petrol-tanks primrose or purple, looped and hooped round with crashbars blooming new bouquets of lights. A few spindly shapes of bikes leaned at odd angles in the collapsing bike-rack, the withered stems of previous summers.

But brighter crimson than roses, the marshalled rows of new 10NT mixers, their tight globes with thin blades inside like new petals: wetly shining with new paint everywhere, so the lined-up machines made one long shape of red. The 5NTs were yellow as a row of blowing tulips; and soft pale blue, the dotted and clustered plaster-mixers. The workshops themselves couldn't be so gay, they weren't so new, though still they receded brightly in asbestos grey with the firm's name spelt across them in large letters. Worlds away, these new factories, from the old battlemented dungeons that rose over the tangled houses to a low dingy weeping sky, with row on row of tiny shut windows not black with transparency but white with bleached dust like wall-eyes; with cruel exposed machinery snatching in the half-light, with no room, and fouled air, and stifling smoke crawling between boards.

Seen from the high office, even the Plate Shop was no more

than a wide plain grey shed, endlessly long. Yet, it had its
shock: its huge end-wall was splitting down the middle. Two
house-high doors were sliding. The hairline crack between
them widened, and little blue figures of men came out.

Round the side of the shop, a gigantic lorry progressed.
The cab itself was built like a tank; and continuous across the
back of the trailer ran rows of wheels like mill-stones. The
gathering men gave way, the lorry crawled across the opening
doors and stopped. The brown desert surface of the trailer
caught the sun like a dirty lake.

The dark gap between the doors stretched to a square, and
tiny shapes of men, small blue flames with red points for
heads, flickered across the space in front. Gradually, barely
seen, beyond benches, machines, and drums, something
monstrous was advancing. There was a green gleam in the
shadows: the factory waited.

*

In the shop, all the platers had stopped work to watch the
hopper leave. So slowly it moved, and silently, the green
hugeness. As it inched up towards the roof it rotated slowly,
and the large yellow letters round it gradually spun out of
sight, then crept back one by one. Hanging from slender
chains, it floated gently like a vast airship towards the
gleaming frame of sky that reached from floor to ceiling at
the end of the shop. So much work and time had gone into it,
the men watched it go as if it were the iron heart of the shop
now being extracted. Clyde, with a serious face, walked
behind and below it as though he himself held this mountain
of iron in mid-air by an effort of will.

On the threshold of the shop a large drying-drum, up-
ended, barred the hopper's path. Clyde shouted, cautious, but

in any case the crane-driver had seen it. The crane stopped and hung for a moment, then swung slowly back again. There was a whirring and grinding of machinery overhead, then once more the hopper climbed, soaring slowly into the wide girder-lined roof of the shop. The yellow letters crept out of sight and back again.

It stopped and hung, and the men debated round Clyde, 'It'll clear the drum now.' 'Come and stand here, it'll just catch it,' 'You come here, matey, it'll sail over clear as houses.' All the angles were unusual, they couldn't decide. The crane-driver himself, looking down, couldn't be sure what was higher than what. To be on the safe side, he raised the hopper again, and advanced.

There came a low, huge musical clang that throbbed and echoed at the bottom of hearing. It continued as the hopper swung clear vibrating, like a great new-cast bell humming over their heads. Everyone heard, or rather felt it, except for the crane-driver up among his whirring cogs. He saw the hopper rotate a trace, unexpectedly, and thought: the pincers are slipping, he prayed they'd hold. But the angles of things below were not right, and the platers down below were waving and dancing. Clyde stood bawling in the centre of the floor. The crane-driver stopped the crane.

Very slowly came the hopper's returning swing. The platers moved clear. Though the crane had stopped the hopper continued forward. As it grazed the drum again a deeper scraping clang resounded, a subterranean quaver, while the drum tilted gradually till it leaned like the funnel of a ship.

Everyone breathed out as the hopper moved on, coming clear of the drum. The drum, though, stayed leaning for a moment, irresolute. Then it too swung back, but it did not swing straight. It turned slowly on its circular base with a quiet, dull, grinding noise. All the Plate Shop watched as, in its strange, airy, slow-motion way, it rotated and heeled over.

With a cacophonous hollow steel echoing it struck a pump that split apart beneath it. The men scattered from the grey rolling shape. A labourer's flat trolley stood in its path and as the drum mounted it the axles snapped, its timbers burst, and the metal sheets stacked on it burst outwards, forwards, downwards, clashing, clattering, shattering all at once.

Where the stack and trolley had disappeared the drum lay motionless as a stranded whale, in a thin eddying smoke of dust.

The men looked up, but the great cone only hung there, unhurt, unscratched, half in the sunlight, light as a balloon against the sky. Everything was still.

'Lias Trigg went up to the drum and with his heavy-duty boot gave it a reverberant booming kick. 'Look at the bugger – not a dent. *There's* yer British steel!'

*

After the delay, the cone was eventually to be seen, by any watching from high windows, crawling clear of the shop and seeming to float in the sunlight without support, till the overhead crane itself slid into the light, a khaki colour, not so bright as its load, and a tiny machine in comparison. The cone crept gradually over the wide trailer, stopped, started, the swinging tonnage was delicately manoeuvred, and down in small delicate movements it came, till it rested on the trailer, projecting far out to either side. Now it was settled, planted, it was inconceivable that anything could lift it, or that the huge wheels of the lorry could truly turn with that burden weighing them down. There was more activity, then, evidently, it was ready to go. More men poured out of the shop, gathering round the cone in a blue crowd as if to wish it farewell. And now, with no movement of starting, it was clear that the cone was crawling forward, almost invisibly: yet, steadily, it picked up speed. It showed behind the furnaces, then crossed the yard, gradually overhauling the parked apologies for lorries, till it came to a halt at the gate. There, tiny white dots of police-cars fell in. One of them moved out into the busy road, and evidently all gave way, for the cone very slowly followed after; and now only the head of the cone appeared, sliding behind the terraced chimneys and housetops.

The doors of the Plate Shop closed again, and it was once more just a bleak, long shed. Behind a distant line of rooftops and tiny chimneys, the green shape still moved. Telegraph poles slid as tiny crosses over the top of it, as it steadily continued its relentless snail's pace advance.

*

The platers returned to the Plate Shop with a certain sadness. Jim Ackroyd, an elderly fitter, came in slowly, stooping more than usual. With his much-creased face, the skin like paper that had been screwed up and unscrewed a dozen times, a faded yellow-brown colour; with his yellow-white hair laid across his head like a large tattered feather, while a thin white scrub crept up his chest beneath his half-unbuttoned aged shirt, indeterminate grey of old iron-dust and old oil; in his old boots, with their skin like sandpaper, and his old leather apron that was all gaping oval holes and dingy hanging tatters; he came in, talking sadly, half to himself. 'It's not like it was. We used to have an outing when we finished a job. We used to go and see it on site. We didn't just go to the door and

146

wave goodbye.' He spat at length, then waved his sallow shrunken knobbly hand, like a wrinkled chicken's foot, in mockery: 'Ta-ta, bye-bye,' he croaked.

'It's not yer baby,' a plater scoffed heavily. 'What you want to go miles to see it for? You know what it looks like by now, I reckon.'

A junior welder laughed. 'I'm glad to see the back of it, big old bugger thing.'

'Puh! It's a poor do, just waving bye-bye out of the window.' Again Ackroyd rose up to his toes and stretched a crooked arm, and mockingly waved. 'Ta-ta!'

The platers said different things as they trooped back into the shop, but they all felt: the hopper had a huge displacement. It left a space, like a solid shadow. Dissatisfied, sad, not clear, they dawdled in twos and threes past the fallen drum, where Clyde stood in the last settlings of dust like a statue: solemn, preoccupied, grieved. The men delayed resuming work, but gradually the banging started, in a withering dry heat that rose steadily. Today prepared to be hotter than yesterday.

26

In the heat of the main street, Pethick came to an attractive shady pub and slipped inside. It was almost empty. There was a lingering sour smell of old cigarettes and beer, but he liked the bar with its coloured lights on, and the barman strolling in from time to time through the plastic streamers, hands in pockets, affable. It was strange to Pethick to see white daylight in the pub, reflecting in the wiped tables.

The few men who were there, he didn't know. A coldy snuffling man, with tearful eyes, sat near the fireplace, leaning on his stick, coughing and spitting into the fender. Near him was a little wizened monkey-faced man, his yellow face one pucker of cocked and curling wrinkles. Across the table was a large man, solidly sat, with a gammy leg stuck out before him. The monkey-faced man crouched low over the table, chuckling to himself as though there were some good joke in Pethick's arrival. The other two were thrown out by Pethick, and it needed some moments of hard staring at him, before they could merge him with the furniture and forget he was there.

Pethick leaned against the wall and tried to calculate. Would the dole be enough? Confusedly he drew sums on the shiny table with the beer from the bottom of his glass. But he lost track, he couldn't read the figures in the drying beer and forgot what they were meant to be. His mind was a weak shambles. Of his visit to the Labour Exchange, all he remembered was the way the clerk he was talking to brightened on noticing that the young clerk next to him was making a mistake. Ignoring Pethick, he leaned across to watch the mistake being made—it wasn't his business to interfere, though the guilty clerk was red to the roots—then he straightened, and returned to Pethick, and the interest died in his face. Of course there was no work going—didn't Pethick know how many men were out of work?

The old men had picked up their thread, the gammy leg presiding. 'He had a wife called Florry. She was a lovely woman—'

'I thought her name was Enid,' quavered the coldy man.

The gammy leg gave a testy thud on the floor. 'Her name was Florry. She was a woman from Wiltshire. She had seven daughters.' He paused impatiently, with raised brows, but the coldy man only snuffled. He went on, 'She was a lovely woman. She used to sell hats, she'd go round the country with a basket of old hats, and put these hats on these old dears' heads and say "Oh, you do look nice, dear."'

'Mats?' asked the coldy man.

'Hats.'

'What?'

'Hats, blast it! HATS! Did you hear that? HATS! Oh Christ, the old fool's deaf as a post.'

They were interrupted by the arrival of another old man, slow, stiff-jointed, stooping—but it was a powerful, broad-chested body that stooped and hunched. He ordered his drink in a loud, thick unshaped voice; and he dropped his change, the coins tinkled on the floor. The other old men cocked eyes at each other, nodding and smiling, and the barman, looking on, smiled their way through his cigarette smoke, indifferently falling in with the humour of his patrons. Pethick went over, and picked up the change for the man.

'Thank you, thanks, you're a real gent,' he said thickly. But he was embarrassed and guarded, suspicious of Pethick. He slowly left the bar, the pint-glass shaking in his hand and spilling half its drink. He approached the others.

'How are you?' he asked in his clogged, clumsy voice.

'Oh, all right, all right.' They nodded, twinkling at him, wanting him to go away. The monkey-faced man almost tittered, he could hardly contain his amusement as he crouched down with his back to the man. He knew he was not wanted, and went and sat across the room: there he began a slow interminable attempt to roll a cigarette with his thick difficult fingers, while the brown shreds scattered across the table. Every so often the other old men looked his way, and softly sniggered to each other.

Pethick watched them, seething with pity and contempt. He knew, he wouldn't get a job. He had nothing he could do, his work was finished; and this limbo of derelicts was all the future that he had.

Time, in the empty barren morning, extended. Pethick started cursing Clyde, Hawkins, the platers—till suddenly he was stopped short by a pang, it grew to a piercing hurt, as he found, he missed the factory. What did he ever get from the work he did there? The heat, the racket, men shouting at him, treating him like filth. Yet he found he had a root that had got under the concrete, and unwound in the suffocated soil. Now it was ripped up, its fibres screamed as if an arm or a leg, as if one side of him, were being torn off slowly.

The three men near the fire were falling out. The gammy

leg banged on the floor. 'His name was Hunter! I knew him!'

'His name was Carruthers!' the coldy man insisted, he was making a stand at last.

'His name was Hunter!' thumped the gammy leg. 'He was a red-haired man. He had a little whippet dog. And it was his uncle Billy, that was the last man but one, that was hanged up Picket's Hill!'

''Sright, 'sright,' the monkey-faced man chuckled. 'Little Billy Hunter, got his neck stretched over a woman.'

The coldy man gave in. He sat blowing his nose, his eyes wept. He took defeat badly.

Pethick got up and rushed from the pub. 'Poor old men, poor old men,' he repeated, in scathing exasperated pity.

*

In the centre of the Civic Gardens, Pethick stopped by a stone obelisk with a heavy chain fence hanging round it like shackles. His eye absently ran down the list of names. There was a faint sway of surprise in him, at not finding a certain name. But he remembered where he was: the names he couldn't find, he never would find here. As he walked down a rustling avenue, the great wall of bolted iron that he had built across his mind, to keep out what had happened in other countries, thinned till it was hardly more than a curtain of light rain.

Bright-coloured prams were parked in the dapple, while mothers moved in and out of sunlight exchanging admirations. The low ripple and splash of the unseen stream was always in his ears. And he stood chattering behind the small waterfall, while the dozily patrolling, well-wrapped-up German soldier gazed reflectively at the water, finishing a cigarette. But also he wandered among houses torn open,

151

where people lay at odd angles without faces.

'Morning, Mr Pethick,' a young voice called. He was so startled, he jumped. Fern Jameson, the messenger-girl at the works, came clip-clopping down the avenue. She had a round sparrow-like brown face, a neat small beak of nose, brown eyes. He had studied her with a wistful private appreciation, and when the odd chance came, on her rounds through the shop, he flirted with her, in a lighter way than the official shop style. He was so surprised to see her, not in the works, but here, that he was shaken out of his thoughts—and he leapt out of them, something in him jumped up and snatched the chance of chatting lightly.

She had taken the morning off, to make last preparations for her wedding. They remembered together the last works wedding, which was bought cut-price at a supermarket: the wedding breakfast was a glass of British sherry and half a glass of wine.

Fern had to hurry; but as she pattered away, a glint of wistful shrewd appreciation persisted in Pethick's eye. He was a man. He found this brief surprise of gallantry had done more to restore him, than a great quantity of grieving sympathy from his poor wife could do.

Ironically pursed, saved temporarily, he went on his way.

27

The other time-studiers were out and studying, and Barry sat by himself in the office, listening for Forbes's return. He had heard no quiet snap of a door, and no sound at all except the low rumble and banging from the Plate Shop. But once when he glanced at Forbes's door, he could not take his eyes away. He gazed, suspended. The door was opening very slowly, as if someone on the other side were pushing it softly. But he saw Forbes inside sitting at his desk, evidently unaware that the door was opening, for he never looked up. He did not have the light on, and this was strange because his office was surrounded by offices and needed a light. In the unusual dimness he just sat at his desk as usual, bent forward in attention, his hands touching either side of the blotter. A thin blade of alarm cut through Barry. The faint light in the office hovered in dim pools, and shimmered unevenly over the graphs on the wall, turning them into different graphs. Forbes was draped and striped with shadows as if he were sitting under machinery. His face was lost, and the curious light gave Barry the odd shock of idea that he was looking through plate glass at an office that had been submerged, at a drowned man.

Though Barry was impatient to see Forbes, he became

busy at his desk, jotting with his biro, and disturbing the ammonia prints so they crumpled and crackled. And presently there was a soft, sliding sound, which he knew was Forbes pushing back his chair, and then quiet steps approached, and paused. There was a faint change in the light. Barry looked up, and saw that the door was closed.

Barry let a long minute pass, then went and tapped hesitantly on Forbes's door. He just heard, it was almost inaudible, Forbes's 'Come in.'

Barry entered—a different office. The brilliant bulb was on, and Forbes sat up at his desk, alert and trim.

'Yes, Barry?'

'I wondered whether you had any news yet about Pethick.'

Forbes continued gazing at Barry, as though he were still waiting for the question.

'I wondered—' Barry began again.

'Yes, yes, I heard,' Forbes snapped, shutting Barry up. Then, with purpose, he dug into his paper-clip tray, picked out a plastic Diners Club card, and started reading the small print on the back.

Barry bridled and heated. 'I dare say nothing can be done?'

Forbes half-attended, tapping his teeth with the plastic card; then, briskly, he got up and strode over to the filing cabinets, as if he wanted to step inside them. He stood motionless a moment, looking at Barry with his back, then spun round. 'Is that the question, Barry?'

'Well. It's a question, Mr Forbes.'

Forbes laughed sharply, then said, 'Don't worry, Barry. Everything that can be done, will be done.'

'Yes?'

'Oh yes.'

'That's good,' Barry said, dissolving in uncertainty. They

looked at each other: Forbes was braced and clear, Barry was doubtful and wavering.

'I am glad, Mr Forbes. Pethick will be coming back, then.'

There was hesitation in Forbes's look and he only said, 'Don't worry about it, Barry.'

Then he added, to show he meant well, 'Really, Barry.' He strode quickly to his desk and sat down. Barry saw he was dismissed, and retreated.

In the Time Study office the phone was ringing. Barry picked it up and at once the musical lilt of the blind telephonist said, 'Mr Spurrier?'

'Yes?'

'There's a call come through for you, Mr Spurrier, it's from a woman. She told me her name was Miss Pethick. Wait a minute, I said, there's a man called Pethick works here in the Plate Shop, isn't there? Yes, she said, I'm his daughter. Course, Mr Pethick, he comes from Czechoslo-vakia I think, but this woman, she speaks English ever so well, but she seems nice really. Well, Mr Spurrier, time flies, and we're none of us getting any younger. But I thought she was ever so nice, only a bit hasty. Well, it's that foreign blood, always a bit on the boil isn't it, but I'll put her through to you if you think it's all right.'

'Put her through please, Miss Abbott,' Barry said. But he was perplexed, not wanting to talk to Ewa now. She came on the line, 'Barry? I'm sorry to ring you here.' Barry paused, and there was a click as Miss Abbott, with reluctant conscience, put her phone down. 'No, Ewa, I'm glad you rang.'

She asked, 'Is there anything? I just wondered, I didn't want to ring from home.' There was a low fuzzy crackling on the line, and a noise like someone whistling, but he made out again the timbre of her voice, which he always liked. There was a rustle in it, a something velvetty and too rich, it sounded inside his head.

Barry didn't want that tone to stop. 'Ewa, I've just seen Forbes again. He was in a queer state, I don't know. He said not to worry, everything that could be done, would be done.'

'Oh, that's hopeful, Barry.' Ewa's voice was as close as if the phone-line were two inches long.

Barry had to go on. 'He didn't say your dad would get his job back. I didn't understand. But he didn't say that . . .' Barry was irritated with himself, he couldn't explain as he wanted.

'I'm sorry, Barry, I don't follow.'

'Ewa, I said to Forbes . . .' Barry began, but what did he say? There was so little he could repeat. He stopped, and in the crackling silence on the line, a space expanded as if they stood on opposite sides of an opening chasm.

Barry's unsure voice crumbled his words. 'Ewa, it is hard to get your dad back if the union don't want it. And, I don't know, does he want to come back to this blasted place? . . .' The misconceived attempt faltered and gave out. Remotely he heard her say, 'I expect you're right, Barry. Never mind.'

'Ewa, it isn't clear yet, really it isn't. Forbes was strange . . .'

Ewa said briefly, she evidently wanted to have done, 'I'm sorry, Barry, I've pestered you a lot. Thanks for trying. Really.' She underlined her thanks, which were cold comfort to Barry. He had planted a seed, in pain he heard it grow.

What could he say to recall her?—but while he shilly-shallied, click! He put his own receiver down.

He sat gazing at the oddly shaped plastic box, which was no gateway to anywhere. So Ewa Pethick was removed from his life as her father was plucked from the factory; and he was in and of the factory, he stayed there. That had always been the issue between them. She would tell him she was for

Nature and against machines, and would run down the Time Study for treating the men themselves like machines. He called her ideas, superstition. He believed that in machinery something that had always been in human nature, and nature, was having its own turn at last. It grew like an iron tree: they lived in its branches and couldn't just jump off. But now he was gathering the iron fruit.

To his surprise, as he sat staring blankly at the cream patch of wall over Bert Cherry's chair, his mind flooded with memories and pictures of Ewa Pethick. They were mainly pictures of her shining as she met him with some new idea as to why the Time Study was an iniquitous thing, as she stood braced, leaning back on a firm spring. The memories fell round him as if he had picked up an envelope, and out of it dropped a host of snapshots he had forgotten, surrounding him. They were only glimpses, moments, he was surprised how they affected him. He remembered a time, a year ago, when he was walking down the pavement and, out of the blue, he turned to find her right behind him, silently creeping up on him on her bike, looking up to no good, caught in the act, bursting and sparkling with bad intentions.

He got up and knocked on Forbes's door again. But there was no answer, and when he opened the door, he found the office empty.

He returned to the Time Study office, and hovered. His gaze caught idiotically on Bert Cherry's multi-storey in-tray; on Ted's rubber thimble for turning pages; on his own stopwatch, stopped, staring at him between parted papers like a blind eye on his desk.

He gathered his palette and other equipment, and went quickly to absorb himself in a study, in a shop that was dry, hot like a desert at noon, and steadily heating more.

28

Barry, with his watch and palette, became one speck among a hundred in the hectic business of the shop's day. Outside there was a still dazzling heat, everywhere was hot and bright as if the atmosphere round the works were made of invisible fire. But inside the shop, all the energy the blinding sun poured down turned not to light but to heat. The walls heated up so it was impossible to go near them, the air made a second quivering wall of heat.

Though the doors at either end of the shop stood open, there was not a breath of wind. With the heat, a dust of shavings and filings and gritty crumbs of metal got up. It hung in the air with the oil-vapour, or on the floor was worked and kneaded with oil to a tacky black paste. A thin gritty film shone in hot stickiness on the overheated machinery, dug into the men's itching skin, got into their eyes and made them burn and water. Through the thick brown atmosphere shaking with noise and heat, the jagged bones of the new, half-made hopper loomed and reverberated.

For some men, there was a respite: for presently a lorry left the factory, curiously laden. In the open back of the truck, lounging on the sides and tailboard, were a handful of platers who looked as though they had been specially picked to make

Hercules look like a clerk. Their hair blew like torn birdsnests over faces like jutting crags; they clutched crowbars, and large wrenches propped up their heads. They were laden with ironware, and all, it appeared, to guarantee protection to a lean wispy sandy man in a suit, in glasses, who sat over a suitcase with his back to the cab. Soon they had paused beside the bank: he left them and he returned to them. And now well might he sit abstracted and demure over his suitcase, while the platers scowled about them, for today was pay-day. The works didn't bother with security express, it had its own tradition, and the gloomy concentration, the lock of sinew, the grim thrust of nose and jaw in every direction, said with massive deterrence to any shady onlooker who might wistfully be interested: '*Our* money!'

The traffic-lights changed to green, and with the lorry in rumbling motion again, the men settled more comfortably to the sun and the ruffling wind; delivering to the factory the cargo of rewards.

*

The platers, welders, fitters, even the labourers, could all go outside for a breather when they wanted. But Len Petchey in the Drawing Stores got no rest. The heat in the Plate Shop and the heat outside overlapped in the tiny windowless Stores. Oily red-faced sweating men shouted for drawings and cursed him, sticking in grimy tickets before he had dealt with the man three turns before. The pile of tickets climbed and he worked desperately to catch up, but as he grew hotter and angrier, his memory played him false. Awkwardly lodged on his short step-ladder, he lugged out a drawing from under a great pile on the top shelf, and found when he checked the ticket that he had got the number wrong. Drawings were lost.

Drawings tore as he jerked them out. The men gave him no peace and they gave him no time. If he kept them long, they lost valuable minutes under the Time Study scheme: at first they coaxed and wheedled him. 'Get a move on, Len!' But soon they shouted and the noise went through his head. It was so scorching, scalding hot he couldn't work or even think.

'Clear off, push off, get out of it!' he shouted hoarsely. 'Come back in half an hour if you like.'

'It'd better be here in five minutes, Len,' they muttered. But the drawing was not there in five minutes or in ten, and after half an hour they found he had given them the wrong drawing.

At last the hooter sounded for lunch. He snapped the hatch down and locked it, sat down on his shaky chair, and let all the air out of his lungs. But he couldn't rest, there were continual jerks and starts inside him, and he came to and found himself half way round the tiny office. Where was he going? For which drawing? His mind burned and spun in pieces, he couldn't sit; he went over to his calendar, and gazed at the date. Then, with the thick blue crayon he used for checking tickets, he scratched and scraped it out of sight: it was like an attack, he tore it up in ragged strips.

Afterwards, he gathered his sandwiches, his Thermos and the *Mirror*, took his chair by the scruff of its neck, and sat himself carefully down outside the Stores, with the chair hard against the wall so he could rest his exhausted back on both.

But while he munched cautiously, his mind still paced and turned in the Stores. What quarters they had given him, the RSPCA wouldn't allow it. He'd go and see Stacey, it couldn't be legal to keep a man in such a box. Or he'd shut up shop and walk out, just leave them to it and see how they liked it. In the groove of these thoughts he nodded off, but his dream was no different from his waking. A.43527, B.73645, C.83759, C.97821—what number is it, a 7 or a 1, God only knows. And this one, is it out already, it's got no ticket, now who's taken it, oh blighted sod more bloody work. Treating him like a machine that won't go so they kick it, and he spent his life here, aren't they his mates? Oh my Christ they're all coming, look at their smiling faces, bloody pigs, give me a drawing, oh yes, I dare say, what would you do if I went on strike? And you can clear off before you start! Fucking apprentices! And who's this coming through the middle of them, by Christ if it isn't Foreman Clyde, wonders will never cease, well honoured I'm sure, if Mahomet won't come to the mountain . . . clanking like a dustbin of nuts and bloody bolts, are you carrying the steel stores there, matey? Any old iron! Any old iron ! Why, Foreman Clyde ! Top of the arternune to you too sir, half a tick and I'll touch my fore-lock. Foreman Clyde! I'll clear his remains away. Stop shouting.'

The platers' din faded. He thought he was still in the Drawing Stores, but they looked different. The packed shelves of drawings were only painted on the wall, and a straight line of light ran down this wall, splitting it from top to bottom. Each half was a door opening outwards, and the light on the other side was so brilliant his eyes watered. With a smooth motion he simply ran at the gate, flinging out his arms and jumping, and at the moment that he leapt the doors flew wide apart. He blinked awake, and gazed round him amazed: he was still in the works, but he had never seen it like this, he thought, when alive. The works lorries were rose-red, the curved roofing and all the windows reflected the blue sky; the still air had a deep warmth; and, from the gate, one figure was walking steadily towards him across the dazzling yard. It was, of all people to meet here, 'Lias Trigg: the sun shone on his bald head, he smiled peacefully. He was a long time coming, but eventually he arrived, his face curious and gentle. And he offered, 'Hey up then, old Len. Fag?' But he put the cigarette away, struck by an odd uncertainty and shifting in Petchey's face. He bent over to him and said, gently bumptious, 'Yer a good old boy at heart, why were you so bloody this morning?' There was no response, only the strange falling fading in Petchey's face. Trigg rotated on his heels to look at the yard. 'Yep! It's a good old day, I'n'it?'

Petchey seemed still in trouble. Trigg reached out a large arm and patted him on the shoulder. 'You should take things easy, poor old boy.'

Petchey jumped at the touch as though shot. Trigg stepped back, and two platers strolling past shouted, 'Here, watch it, 'Lias. He bites.'

In an instant, Petchey was in frenzy, 'Who bites? What the hell do you mean? Come back here! '

The platers baited him from a distance, till Trigg interrupted, 'Here, lay off, will you, shut your row ! Poor old chap!' At that Petchey turned on him. 'You keep out of it, Trigg, I can take care of them.'

'Len, slow down, you'll do yourself an injury.'

'Bleeding hell, Trigg, keep out of it, will you? I know you, you're just like them. Clear out, go on, shove off!'

'What yer mean? I took your part,' Trigg cried, but Petchey was trapped in his rhythm, and shouted at all of them to get out. Trigg stalked away, and the two platers followed him, tickled. Petchey watched them from his territory, then he carried his chair into the Drawing Stores and shut himself in. There he let go, he subsided into the chair and ground his dry face in his dry hands.

*

162

In the Plate Shop, men wanting drawings collected at the hatch. They leaned on the wall, or shifted their weight from one leg to the other, and chatted easily. There was no hurry. They knew his moods, and didn't mind having this extra time after lunch to digest and gossip. But eventually they grew impatient, 'What's he doing in there? He's been an age.' In the end, one of the men tapped on the hatch. 'Len? Len!'

There was no reply, and he tapped again. 'Len, are you getting along pretty much all right, old chap?'

After a pause, they heard Petchey shout in a dull voice, 'What's that you want?'

'Is it early closing, mate?' The apprentices chorused 'Why-are-we-waiting?'

They stepped back, expecting the hatch to fly up in vigorous retort. But it didn't, and again they leant close to it, to catch what he said.

From the other side Petchey shouted, 'I'm tidying up!'

'Tidying up? Well, don't do it now, old mate.' The platers were genial and tolerant after lunch.

'I'm putting things in order. You wait till I've tidied up,' he called. The platers looked at each other doubtfully. 'Well, hurry it up, Mrs Mop.'

Some went off to other jobs, others waited, others came. Time passed, and Petchey did not open the Stores. Eventually the platers knocked and rattled on the hatch, and shouted at him again. After a pause, his voice rose querulously, 'I'll come when I'm ready, not before. You clear off.'

At the back of the crowd, a quiet voice exclaimed to a newcomer, 'Screw me! Come and see the stew he's in!' A chuckle crackled dryly like trodden straw.

They heard a deep groan from inside the Stores. 'There isn't room to swing a cat in here.'

Finally several platers lost patience and surged forward. 'Get us our drawings for Chrisake!' Warboys shouted, 'I'm not having this!' and banged on the hatch so it jiggled in its grooves. 'Open this fucking hatch and give us our drawings!' Others joined him, there was a hammering of fists on the wood—which suddenly stopped, at a great shout from inside; but they could not make out the words. They fell back.

'We'd better fetch Clyde.'

The platers blew this way and that, in rising uncertainty, while more came to join them. They loitered, dangling their gaze on the small closed wooden shutter. If they banged on it, it did no good: the man stayed inside shut away as though he were not surrounded by good mates at all, but alone in the dark.

Several platers went off in a group to hunt out Clyde.

29

Clyde was just clanking in through the side-door of the shop when the platers found him. He was sleepy, his body was cumbersome and hot, and as the platers told him what had happened, his eyes attended, while he covered his mouth with his large hand. But at the end, he only said, with a general consideration for the peace of ageing men after lunch, 'Leave him be for now, let him cool off. If he's still there in half an hour, I'll come.' The platers told him that Petchey had already had his half-hour, and more, but Clyde wouldn't listen. He hustled them off to other jobs.

The platers, perplexed, left him for the present. But still, when they were gone, the driller, Strachey, stayed behind. He hovered in the gangway leering and glinting, all his long yellow boniness trembling and coiling with some rare bad news he had for Clyde.

'Afternoon, Mister Clyde,' he shouted. Clyde watched him with dry, unforthcoming eyes.

'Will you be going away then, Mr Clyde? South of France, perhaps? Timbuctoo?'

Clyde's stare narrowed, Strachey leaned close to him. 'Or you could take an allotment, have you thought of that? You could flog stuff.'

In heavy contempt, Clyde asked, 'What's eating you, Strachey?'

Strachey's eyes widened, his mouth made an 'O', he exclaimed, 'Oh, don't you know? I'd have thought they'd have told you first of all. They should have, shouldn't they?' Through his pantomime, tightly, he grinned at Clyde.

'Tell me what, for Christ's sake?'

'Oh, about the new Foreman, 'course.'

Clyde's brow slightly rose, but that was all. He was an old hand, with massive weariness he said, 'What are you on about, Strachey?'

'There's to be a new Foreman. Didn't you know?' Clyde scoffed at the idea. 'Who then, eh?'

Strachey was all bewilderment, 'Search me. How should I know that?'

Clyde went on, in heavy indifferent scorn, 'Who says there's to be a new Foreman? Did Stacey tell you over coffee, then?' He moved on, leaving Strachey disappointed. He would betray nothing, his face was impassive, but chalky. Immediately he was consumed not so much with the news, as with a spasm of helpless loathing of Strachey, he wanted to smash him down. But his experienced body walked him solidly clear.

*

His fury with Strachey soon burnt out. For the news Strachey brought him, at first Clyde only felt a weary sinking inside himself. So: it had happened. He was surprised he wasn't surprised. The news just came home, bare, bleak, like hearing the truth after a long prevarication.

He knew what he must do. Strudwick, Forbes, Stacey, they had some explaining to do. They hadn't seen the last of him, it was no such easy job to chuck him out of the window. But he couldn't go now, he was too broken up. Also there was the whole afternoon shift to sort out, he had to be everywhere at once, there were so many things to do. It was too cruel: the news came when he didn't even have a moment in which he could take it in. He couldn't think because the men were at him all the time, but also he couldn't listen to what they said. He was like a machine smashed over and all its wheels knocked out of mesh, spinning crazily, stopped dead, driving nothing, except for some little spinning cog deep in his works which never stopped asking, who did it, who's at the back of it? The bosses, the Time Study, the union, his men, it could be all of them. He turned and turned, getting nowhere, till he was jaded, sick, almost out of his mind. His brain burned like a live coal they had stuck into his head.

Then a plater came to him who wasn't hectoring and truculent like the others, but just in trouble, deferential, begging for help. It was, of all people, King Farouk, standing all unbuttoned and confounded, mopping and sopping the glistening beads on his bald head. And all his trouble was that something had jammed in the cutters, and they weren't working right. The simple request to put a machine to rights came to Clyde like a drop of fresh water. His old fascination revived: he heaved his worries to one side, and strode off with Farouk.

They arrived at the offending machine. Clyde walked round it, eyeing it severely. He tried the controls cautiously, he looked inside it. Then he reached in, and pulled and pressed at the mechanism: and that was that, he had found the trouble.

'Soon fix this.' He proceeded to empty his pockets on to the bed of the machine: out came wrenches, screwdrivers, pliers, gauges, scribers, spanners, it was like a toolmaker's jumble-sale. But he found the spanner he wanted and reached into the machine: and there he stayed, motionless, half in the engine, while his face slowly reddened with strain. He came out panting. He took another spanner and reached in again, but still it didn't work. 'Oh what's the matter with the bloody fucking thing, it won't undo, it won't budge.' Now his thick arm had disappeared to the shoulder and his face was swollen, red, getting steadily more desperate, till he looked as though he had got tangled in the works and was struggling to get out.

Farouk said nervously, 'Should you try the seven-eighths, Mr Clyde?'

'The seven-eighths! Oh you bloody fool, what use is that?' But presently Clyde fished out the seven-eighths and lunged into the machine with it. It didn't work either, and he bawled curses at Farouk. In the mood he was in now, he couldn't repair the machine, but he couldn't leave it alone. He started the motor while he was still half inside it: Farouk stared aghast, he could be torn apart. The engine grated and shrieked, and now there was no way to tell whether the machine was being tortured by the man, or the man being eaten by the machine. When Clyde got clear his whole arm was red and scratched and the beads and smears of black-red blood were hardly different from the skeins and loops of black oil all round it, so it looked still as though he had ripped it, torn and damaged, from a furious mouth.

'Try it,' he said.

'I'm not sure it's mended, Mr Clyde.'

'It'd bloody better be! ' Clyde snapped, and he insisted: so a sheet of metal was put into the blades, which jolted and bleated and didn't cut the metal.

'You bloody fool, you're putting it in wrong!'

'It won't go, Mr Clyde,' Farouk gasped, while at the same time he gave the metal another shove with his stomach, and the cutters sent up a piercing howl.

'For Christ's sake!' Clyde snatched the plate himself, and pushed it between the blades: they shrieked, no go. He stopped swearing, and now, inwardly, he prayed to the machine to work. He realigned the plate and pushed it in, the machine grated and screamed, and now it cut, he gave it no option, his great strength insisted, but the blades snagged and tore the metal, there was no clean cut but a torn jagged rip of prickled and cockled iron.

After a pause, sadly and simply, he said, 'You'd better get the engineer.' He retreated. Even his machines betrayed him now.

*

From a neglected corner where spare steel was stacked, Clyde looked out at his shop. A plater pored over a drawing; two men wound metal through the rolls like house-wives at a mangle; a gang of men hammered together, the hammers rising one after the other in one regular wave.

He watched them all and thought, he didn't need to be there: he had fretted about the work of the shop, but it all went on anyway, what did it matter if he were there or not? As he watched them he woke to what normally he scarcely heard at all, the deafening noise his shop made. From lathes, drills, hammers, presses and motors went up the constant shrieking and battering and grating and roaring. To it bodies swung and hurried, huge bits of metal rose and fell or hovered forward out of smoke while blue weld crackled and flared. It was all outside him now, it hardly made sense any more. The torrent of roaring noise drove on and on through his head like an avalanche of iron boulders jumping and dancing down an endless mountain, its racket would crack the ears of the world for ever: but he was nothing to it now, he was so much old scrap, discarded. His head split with the din, he staggered out of his shop.

30

Clyde paused in the blinding yard. He must see management right away, but he was unprepared, unready. Where could he go? He started for the offices: but in front of him was the foundry, two huge irregular hooded towers of brown rust soared out of the sprawled and piled heaps of scrap-iron. Clyde was premier foreman, but the foreman of the foundry was a buddy and a peer, Clyde would go and see him.

He picked his way through the slag-heaps of scrap, then through a dead forest of castings. Mixer-bowls, and all sizes and types of wheel, newly cast, were piled up all round him in close columns taller than he was, the new-cast metal a matt leaden grey, the older castings bright russet or blood-red with rust.

The foundry itself, when he got there, was grey, spacious, airy. The floor was covered with moulds, low square boxes

171

laid out like an expanse of gardening frames. In all the boxes, overflowing from them, and ingrained in the blue clothes and white skin of the foundrymen, who picked their way carefully between the boxes like gardeners, was the grey sand used for moulding: a dead, ashen, unimaginably sterile tilth. Jameson, the foreman, a huge gentle man who always kept clean, pink and fresh in the foundry grime and fume, was kneeling down by one of the frames, pressing his thumb into the rubbery compound of sand. Gas had been pumped through the sand to harden it, but still it wasn't hard enough.

Jameson saw Clyde and came over. He had a large head shaped like a child's, with a bulging forehead, and he walked with his head down like a buffalo, and his innocent-friendly blue eyes looking up to see the way he was going. He looked like a man made to be taken advantage of, but Clyde went in awe of him. The foundry was the hardest shop to run, they were always having fights, and all that happened then was that Jameson's pink face flushed, so his blue eyes sparkled more blue and flower-like, while he picked up the combatants slowly and chucked them into different heaps of sand.

With a rough grate in his voice, Clyde asked, 'Have you got any odd jobs, then?'

'How's that?'

'Don't you know? They're taking me off the Plate Shop, I expect they'll make me a director.'

Jameson looked at him seriously, and his face steadily deepened till he looked as though he might weep sympathy. 'Who did you see, Edward? Stacey?'

Clyde scoffed. 'Huh! No such luck!'

'You saw Strudwick, did you?'

Clyde's hands made small annoyed movements, 'Oh, I heard about it, don't worry.'

'Who told you about it, Edward?'

In extreme irritation, Clyde muttered, 'Who was it? Oh, one of my men, what's his name, Strachey it was.'

'Strachey? But Edward, you saw management, didn't you?'

Clyde looked away, to the furnace. Now it was the mature features of his own face, the fleshy nose, the large cheeks, the heavy undersling of jowl; heated, swollen and red as they were; with their irritated surface softly rough like broken cork; that shaped in helpless curves and made his face look: boyish. He didn't answer.

Jameson gazed at him, grave and puzzled, in a way that infuriated Clyde. 'Well, but Edward, I mean . . . how do you know it's true?'

Clyde turned on him in fury. 'Oh, it's true all right, don't you worry about that. I know it's true I know the buggers! I know them'

They paused; Jameson, solemn-faced, avoided looking at Clyde. Then he had to attend elsewhere. His charge-hands were making a final inspection of the moulds, and he watched them do it as though he were seeing through their eyes. He returned to Clyde, but he didn't press further, Clyde should know the situation. Eventually he said, hot with indignation, 'What gets me about this, Edward, is that they let this out in the shop, before they told you. That's disgusting. Oh, I call that, poor.'

Clyde stared at him. After the pause, he was irritated that Jameson had decided so easily to believe—Yes, it was true, Clyde was sacked. How did Jameson know? He had only seen Strachey—perhaps it wasn't true at all. But at the same time Jameson's indignation caught like pestilence, it blazed and consumed him. To hear it first from one of his men! His mind blacked out with seething blood.

The foundrymen called Jameson away, the furnace-door was being raised. A large man in overalls, with layers of leather tunic and apron on top, with a hood on, and goggles over his eyes, was cranking up the gate. He poked inside with a long bar, and dazzling iron ran out. Pairs of men came through the foundry, carrying the iron in ladles: they tipped the ladles, and the iron ran in thin streams like milk into the hole in the centre of each mould, till yellow bubbles of it stuck out at the airholes round the sides. The covered man at the furnace-door stooped over the stream, raking it.

Clyde stumbled out of the foundry, his mind torn between the thought that perhaps it wasn't true, Strachey had it wrong, and the other thought, that they had told his men before they told him. It burned in his mind worse than the sacking itself, as though a spit of the white-hot metal had splashed on to his head and ate through the bone to his brain.

As soon as he was clear of the foundry, before he could think what he would do, a gang of men from his own shop caught him. Petchey was still holding them up, and they needed new drawings for the new hopper: he was holding all of them to ransom, they couldn't wait longer, Clyde had to come now. Clyde stared at them with wide dancing eyes, but what could he do?

'I'll come, I'll come,' he said. They swept him into the Plate Shop.

31

When Clyde was still far from the Drawing Stores, a ragged path opened among the platers, leading to the hatch. As he walked towards it, he faltered, his head swam, he hardly knew whether he was looking across the shop, or whether he was looking down a long shaft with the hatch at the bottom, and everything else falling towards it. Men and machines were spinning as they fell, sucked round in the whirlpool, but he could see also that the movement was only an odd sick tremble or shiver running through everything. He shook his head jerkily, he was afraid he would pass out. But now he had arrived and was aware of his own quiet, massive clanking. As he walked through the platers, who quietly slid out of his way, it was like walking back into his old state and importance. Everything hung on him still.

Without hesitation he went up to the hatch, stood beside it a moment as though listening, then called, 'Len, open up, will you? It's Mister Clyde. I want to talk to you.' He spoke with his old authority, the large sound of it was all he had left. But also there was a low throb in his voice, of one ageing man in difficulties to another.

There was no noise from inside the Stores, and outside also the platers watched and waited, dead silent, as if they still had faith in Clyde, in a kind of superstition. Perhaps the new silence would carry his words through to Petchey, for no one else had so stilled the general barracking.

There was a quiet rustling inside the Stores. The hatch shook, then it was lifted and hooked up. The platers closed in, and caught in their faces the gust of burning air that broke from the enclosed office. Petchey stared back at them like the ember of someone burnt alive. It looked odd that he still wore his buff tunic with its darned elbows and frayed cuffs, for the skin of his face was dried-out and looked so brittle it could crack, there were stark red stars on his cheeks, his eyes were wide-open in a dry staring fever.

Clyde was aghast and moved to see him. 'Len,' he began gently, and at once Petchey cut across him,

'You mind your business, Clyde. Leave me be. I'm getting things straight.' But then he crumpled down on the counter, and gasped, 'Oh Christ, it's hot in here.'

'Len, come out of there, have a breather,' Clyde said. Petchey was up at once. 'Oh yes? Come out, you say, do you? Tell me then, what'll happen to the drawings if I come out of here?'

'Come out and get some air, Len. I'll ask old Jim Strutt, up the Offices, if he'll come and do the drawings and that. Take it—'

'Oh yes? Jim Strutt, is it? And what about tomorrow, and the next day? I know your game. You want to put someone else in here. Eh? Eh?'

Clyde trembled, his face worked, but he only said, 'Len, stay there if you want to. Stay there. But give my men their drawings.'

'Ah well, old Clyde, they'll have to wait.' He looked round at the platers. 'Do you hear that, then, old mates, you can sodded well wait till I'm ready. This is my office, and I'm here.'

A plater jeered, 'Is this your famous strike, then?'

In a heavy half-choked voice Clyde said, 'Look, Len, take it easy. What is it you're after? What do you want us to do?'

'Oh, that's your tone is it now? Look, Clyde, do you know how long I've worked here?'

'Len, we've been here . . .'

'Oh, don't you start that, I've been here a bloody sight longer than you, old boy. I come here first, I was a boy of fifteen, I come here then . . . boy of fifteen . . .' There, so soon, he lost his thread.

Clyde gazed at the older man with a gentle energy of fellow-feeling. What else could Petchey say, but that he had been in the works ever since? He hated it now but he had nothing else, so he stayed on.

The platers were quiet. Clyde said, 'Look, Len, why don't you let Josh come in, my man Josh. You know I won't let Josh go for good.'

At once Petchey was back in his anger. 'Oh, you keep out of it, you and your merry men, Clyde. I know what help means from you, my old hot potato.'

Clyde's bursting temper began to give way. 'Oh bleeding hell, man, what do you want us to do?'

'What! Clyde! Don't you raise your voice to me! Keep clear, get away, go on.'

Clyde could hold back no longer, at the hoarse racked top of his voice he shouted, 'Oh for Christ's sake, man, what the fucking hell is the matter with your mind? Get those blasted drawings out! Get them now! Do you hear? Blasted get on with it, oh you stupid old blasted old old bloody old fool!' Clyde stopped, he had to. His throat had dried as though he were eating straw, he was as close to tears as if he had been shouting for pity. Petchey stared at him, dazed. He moved uncertainly, reached up, and

Snap! Down came the hatch, like the blade of a guillotine, hitting the sill with a crack that ripped through the shop like a shot.

Clyde snatched clumsily at the handle and tried to jerk the hatch up. But Petchey had hooked it down, it only rattled, and Clyde's thick muscular hand trembled as it tugged, to no purpose.

Clyde straightened and stepped back. 'Get Surtees,' he shouted. 'Tell him to bring his crow.'

'Wait a bit.' 'Poor old boy,' the platers murmured. Clyde ignored them, and just waited, staring at the hatch.

Surtees arrived. He was the shop blacksmith, a broad and deep-bodied five foot eight, like a short giant. He was a character, he wore scorched and charred grey flannels, and a black singlet that scarcely hid a tangle of sinews like plaited hawsers. His skin was burnt brown, with black smears and marks all over, as though he himself had been passed through the furnace every day for decades. He wore horn-rim glasses behind which his eyes were large and dark. He had a lit cigarette over one ear, and a much crumpled trilby hat set askew on his burnt head.

'Surtees,' Clyde called, 'That poor old boy's stuck in there. We've got to break in.' Surtees looked at him with his heavy enlarged eyes, modestly ready to do any breaking that was needed.

Clyde shouted, 'Do you hear that, in there? You open up now, or we'll bust in. OK?'

There was no sound from behind the hatch. Clyde nodded to Surtees, who raised his crow like a heavy lance, and swung it into the shutter. There was a sharp crack of sound, the wood cracked from top to bottom. The platers stared at the jagged yellow line in the dark brown wood. Surtees swung back for a second blow, when a dry voice rose:

'You listen here. I've got a box of matches in here, and if you try that again, the whole bloody issue goes up in smoke.'

Surtees lowered his crowbar. The platers shouted, 'Ain't you hot enough in there as you are?' 'Open up, for Chrisake!' There was no answer, and a silence of bewilderment expanded round the tiny hatch, till it was interrupted by the noise of King Farouk's cutter, across the shop, as he forced the steel in and the whirr of iron abruptly climbed to a piercing shriek that rose and fell in waves.

Clyde gazed at the hatch, his swollen face crimson, furrowed. His strong hands weakly pattered his sides, his iron-ware nervously tinkled and chattered.

As if, after Petchey, he had to follow suit, he walked down the shop gangway, climbed the staircase to his office, and slammed the door as he went inside.

32

Clyde closed his eyes and leaned back on the door: alone at last. But he was not alone. In the centre of his vision, when he opened his eyes, was his clerk Josh, with his back to him, ordering cards. The large back was motionless like a sack, the soiled oatmeal jacket nearly burst across the bent, fat shoulders. Clyde wanted him gone, but was too worn out to get rid of him. He turned in the office, in an irritation of restriction, swearing about Petchey. Eventually he said, 'You heard the latest, then, Josh?'

Josh turned, there was a flutter in his thick glasses. 'I'm out, Josh. The boot. I've got the sack.'

Josh's glasses, in the puckering red face, glittered at Clyde like two blank coins.

'After all these years, Josh! After all I've done! Chucked out for scrap, out on my ear, in the street! What do you say to that?'

He breathed tremblingly for some moments, then began again, 'Well, Josh, I know who's behind it. Do you know, I was going half out of my mind, thinking it might be people in the shop. But I know who it is—it's Forbes, and the Time Study. They're the ones. It's because I know too bloody well how this place works—while I'm still here, all they are is the icing on the bleeding cake. So I've got to go. But dammit, Josh, when I think what I've done for this blasted place, I've put heart and soul into it time out of mind, they've never had such a foreman as I was, I know that. And now what'll happen to it? It'll all go to rack and ruin. You remember the machines we used to make here, they were lovely! Weren't they, Josh, they'd last till doomsday. Now look at the filthy rubbish we sling out, it drives me mad to look at it. Save a minute here, dearie, save a minute there, that's their whole carry-on, break it up, smash it down, all to bits and pieces, little titchy scraps, however bad the work gets. Because time's money, and money, money, money, that's all they think about, nothing else, and this place isn't here only to make blasted fucking money and nothing else at all, is it? Is it? Oh, if I had my way, what I'd do to them, I'd smash them! Filthy white maggots, filthy grubs in my shop!'

His blazing face hung over Josh like a burning planet, he raged on and his bitter tones grated and scraped the inside of Josh's head, till Josh was suddenly carried back to something he had seen when he was a boy, on the farm where his father worked, when a cow went mad. The two cowmen in their jerseys and wellingtons had tied a rope round the cow's horns, and one end of the long rope was tied to a tree, the other end they were trying to fix to a stake wedged in the ground. The cow was throwing its head all the time, its eyes rolled, its mouth foamed, and the noises it made were like nothing in nature. As it shook its head, it tore its horns, and all round the tied horns the blood ran freely, so it looked as though the horns would be uprooted in the struggle. He still saw the two men's faces, frightened, appalled, clenching their mouths as they worked at the ropes. This came back to Josh, as Clyde went on until he lost speech, and banged and punched on the desk so the paper towers slid and tumbled, spanners and wrenches clattered down, and clouds of yellow and green tickets flew up like old leaves in a gale; they swirled and fluttered round him, and settled on the grubby floor. Clyde's face flared up, so changed Josh scarcely saw it as a face, but as something skinned, convulsed, consumed. He couldn't find Clyde in it.

He stood up, and with a sudden power he bellowed hoarsely, 'Mr Clyde! Sit down!'

Confronted with this tall and shouting Josh, with the alarm wide open in his face, Clyde was amazed. He was completely thrown. Slowly, gazing with a waking worry, he sat down. He shook and shifted, several times he tried to speak, but no words came. Then, with a slow shrug, whatever it was that held him upright, gave. His powerful stout body slowly sank against the bench, and he just sat, dazed.

After a long interval, Josh asked, in his normal quiet pursy voice, 'What did Stacey say, Mr Clyde?'

'Stacey, Stacey? I heard it in the shop, Josh. I heard it first from one of my men. Strachey.'

'Strachey?' Josh's plump hard brows compressed. 'You're going to see management, Mr Clyde?'

But there, Clyde switched off. He only creaked round on his buckled chair, and Josh saw he could not get through to him now.

Josh brooded, and from time to time glanced at Clyde. What Clyde saw through the window, he didn't know, but presently a string tautened in Clyde. He sat up, and then in a congested, soft, absent voice he said through the window, 'Hello, old chap. Are you getting along pretty well?'

Josh blinked, and looked at Clyde in alarm. But presently a little tit hopped on the sill, and balanced there on its delicate hairline legs, while its head jerked from side to side. Clyde said, 'Hey, old chap, you're looking prime. Stay there, now. Don't move.' Josh was tickled to see that even in aberration, Clyde was still the foreman, and told the bird what to do.

There was a rustle of paper, Clyde's hand was stealthily busy under the bench while he gently inquired how the bird was keeping, in a tone he couldn't use with people any more. Surreptitiously he broke the crumb of his sandwich, and flicked grains of bread across the sill. Then he returned to full foreman. He had given the bird enough of his time, and he made a brisk kindly movement with his hand so the bird flew off.

Clyde looked at Josh, and breathed out wearily, 'The scrap-heap—that's all I'm good for now.'

'I expect you'll go and see management, Mr Clyde.'

Clyde nodded heavily. He saw Josh was asking the question Jameson had asked, why didn't he go to the bosses straight away? He was too tired to fight it off any more. He knew he didn't go because he was frightened. And he was frightened because he knew in his bones that what Strachey had said was true. How did he know it was true? With a kind of collapsing within him, a giving way of something enormous that had resisted, he dully reiterated this question as though he met in it, his conscience. With this, a weight was lifted from him, but with the lifting of it he felt more tired than he had ever felt in his life.

He got up. 'I'll see them now. I should have seen them before.' He left the office. When he was gone, Josh lowered himself on to the floor and, wheezing painfully, started to collect the scattered and strewn, crumpled and trodden-on job-cards.

At the bottom of the steps, Clyde glanced across the shop,

and saw more men gathered at the Drawing Stores. Strudwick had arrived now, and stood before the hatch, responsible and determined, while the platers brought him up to date. Clyde inspected with fierce derision his silvery grey trousers with a crease like a razor, his white shirt spotless like a visiting angel, rolled back on plump pink fore-arms, his general gingery redness like a walking hot flush.

Who should he see? He couldn't see Strudwick, in front of his own men. To his surprise and dismay, he found himself preferring, of those available, Forbes. 'I'll beard him in his den!' Forbes was the enemy.

Before Strudwick and the others noticed him, he hurried out of the shop.

33

Strudwick strode up to the hatch, and his firm plumpness looked hard as cement. 'Petchey, can you hear me? It's Mister Strudwick here. They tell me you're in a spot of bother. So I've come to say that if you tell me straight out what the trouble is, I'll try and do something about it, p.d.q. I can't say more than that.'

He had spoken firmly, he even waited firmly, tight in concentration, as if he were a bomb which he himself, by willpower alone, just kept from exploding. 'I can't hang around,' he called again, balancing in his voice the remains of goodwill with the stirrings of reproach. 'Petchey, the men here, they need those drawings. I ask you, is it fair to hold them up, if your grievance is with us? Tell us what the trouble is, and we'll sort it out. They say you're on strike. Well, if you're on strike, you should be ready to negotiate. That's the point of strikes, that's how you get something. So, Petchey, if you want to negotiate—I'm here.'

It seemed Petchey didn't want. And Strudwick grew depressed at the indignity of haranguing a closed wooden serving-hatch.

'Petchey, we can't wait around, there's a lot on today. If you don't open that hatch—I'm sorry, but you'll be fired, here and now. We'll have no choice. But we don't want to fire you, we want to help you. So—come on, old man, open up.'

But even now there came no answer. Strudwick turned away, muttering loudly in annoyance, 'Ee, it's no damn good at all, he can't hear a word I'm saying.'

'Well, something must be done,' he said, and he stood a moment, firmly considering.

'Right!' he said, as if the solution, like a ripe fruit, had dropped into his hands. 'Where's the nearest phone?'

The platers looked at each other. 'Clyde's . . .' they began.

'Never mind, I'll go to my office. You men get back to your benches. Don't hang around here. I'll soon see to this.'

The men were bewildered, but Strudwick shone, and set off through the shop with the bouncy walk of an athlete. The men dawdled and hung, some of them drifted back to their benches.

Strudwick sped down the corridors, and the doors hurtled open on each others' heels. He slammed into his office, slipped into his chair, drew a quick breath of refrigerated air, planted his elbows on the table, and picked up the phone.

He rang Clyde's clerk Josh, and told him to get the numbers of all the drawings now in the shop, and the numbers of all the drawings that were needed. He rang the Time Study Office, and told them to list the drawings just processed. He rang the Drawing Office, and told them to get the numbers from Josh, and make new prints from the original tracings. He got so carried away, he rang up the Drawing Stores itself, but he got short shrift there. He had a setback, when the Drawing Office rang to say that their ammonia-print machine was not working, they had been meaning to repair it for some days. But Strudwick rang up the print-machine firm there and then, to find out when in emergency they could make the repair, and when they could deliver a replacement machine. He even rang another firm, to see if he could hire their machine. He told everyone briskly, clearly, courteously, firmly, exactly what he wanted; and when he had done that, he sat back in his chair, and breathed in with zest the glacial air in his office.

Throughout the works a sense of purpose revived, and people hurried past each other in different directions. Everywhere there was movement and urgency, as Strudwick's tasks were delegated to a hundred idle hands.

So all moved. And yet, the print-machine couldn't be repaired, and the firm who made it couldn't come for a fortnight, and couldn't lend another, and no one else could. And when he knew the numbers of all the drawings that were needed, and when these numbers were set out clearly in ascending order in their several categories, still it was not the same as having the drawings themselves. None the less, there were revelations. The chief of the Drawing Office discovered with amazement that his predecessor had left the original tracings in a shambles, it was the devil's own job to make sense of them, while a number of the tracings had actually been lodged in the Drawing Stores itself, and were still there. Furthermore the chief of the Drawing Office let it be known that the main blame for today's troubles lay with the Time Study, who kept coming to look up old drawings, and took them away, and never brought them back. What they did with the drawings he didn't know, he hardly liked to imagine, indeed they had made his life such that only an executive of genius could have stuck it so long. And on the other hand again, the Time Study Office found on inspection that although they had supposed they had only twenty or so drawings on the premises, as it turned out they did actually have two hundred, and it indicated the kind of chaos that obtained in the Drawing Office, that these drawings had never been sent for. But as to whether these two hundred drawings were the drawings that were wanted in the Plate Shop now —frankly no, they weren't, they were other things entirely. But two of the drawings that were needed now, they did have.

One by one the reports came in, and the brisk men had nowhere else to go, and kicked their heels awaiting orders. After the best part of an hour they were all at a standstill again. Strudwick was no nearer solving the problem, though he did indeed now know, with a finer exactness, precisely how bad the situation was. And the platers gathered again at the Drawing Stores, in greater numbers than before.

34

Following the collapse of the Strudwick initiative, the platers outside the Stores were left sitting or squatting as best they could on whatever benches, boxes or machines were available. In the centre, 'Lias Trigg sat on a trolley, stripped to the waist, his plump large body, smeared here and there with oil, glistening all over in support of his polished bald head. He was being the life and soul, but in spite of that the plater just behind him, Hopper, had nodded off, leaning in a heap against a girder. The hot dew on all of them caught in glistening bulbs among his rough-cut stubble, and from his open mouth came a painful tearing wheezing snore, it was hard to believe he could really sleep and also make this noise of pain. Notwithstanding the regular interruptions, Trigg was favouring them with his reminiscences of Clyde. The smallest things came back to him, he remembered even the cream biscuits that Clyde used to bring in each afternoon, his wife did them up for him in a paper bag.

'So one day, I had a word with old Josh, and he brought me them biscuits. And do you know what I did? I opened them up, I scraped out the cream, and I put in lathe grease.'

'Lathe grease, 'Lias?!' Nutty Saville exclaimed. An apprentice lounging on the floor cried out, 'I bet that made him run.'

Trigg was not abashed. 'Ah, do you know what happened, though? Josh told me after. Clyde come in, he dunked those biscuits in his tea, and do you know, he ate them, every one, and he never even noticed.'

The older platers smiled on cue, Trigg grinned ruefully, and Hopper behind him gave a long rasping snore. Jim Dawson, standing up, scuffed his boot on the concrete floor and muttered impatiently, 'Christ Almighty, when's he going to open up?'

George Reynolds, the elderly plater who knew all the jobs by heart, was passing by, and he stopped to bestow on the group a deep, ironic, gratified smile. Then he proceeded up the shop, and grandly, in good view of all of them, he continued marking out, while his bonus multiplied.

Victor Watts came back. He had been to the Foundry to see the father of the boy injured yesterday. 'How is he, Vic?' the platers asked.

'I seen Steve Carter,' Watts told them, 'He said the lad is all done up in plaster and metal from here to here.' He pointed from his neck to his finger-tips.

'Will he have the use of his arm, Victor?'

'God knows. He said, they'll have to wait. But Steve said, he doesn't say anything, he just lies there. Steve said it broke his heart more to see him all done up like that than when it happened.'

The platers shook their heads.

There was a heavy crash inside the Drawing Stores; they looked round, startled.

'What's he up to in there?'

Presently there was another crash, then no more.

The platers looked at each other in consternation, they were past trying to make contact with Petchey. Nutty Saville opined, 'You know, 'Lias, I don't reckon Mackworth Crowley will keep him on, not after this. I reckon he's blotted his copy-book good, with this.'

Another said, 'Yes, well, we don't none of us know whether we'll be kept on, do we, my old son of a gun?' Then the whole uncertainty leapt to the surface. Several platers attacked the union for not doing more. Hawkins was up in arms at once. 'What's that? Is he criticizing the union?' In the sweltering heat, they were all ready for a fight; but 'Lias Trigg poured oil. 'All right, all right, old mates, what odds does it make, anyway, for Christ's sake? What do you expect? Either we hang on here till we drop, like this old boy'—he thumbed at the Stores—'or we go out in the cold like the poor bleeder yesterday.' He said it like one of his jokes, and smiled about him with every curve of his rubbery face.

At the reference to Pethick, one or two men looked across uneasily at Wally Reed, Pethick's friend, who sat by himself on the outskirts of the group. He had held aloof from the others since the union meeting, but he was unused to doing this, and unhappy. He hunched awkwardly, he smoked nervously, ceaselessly, and every so often he looked wistfully towards the main gang.

Reg Barrett, from the brake press, hurried up to them excited, wiping his head with rapid dabs. 'Is he still in there?'

'Hasn't shown his face.'

'My Christ! Hey, you know what?'

He was so excited, he couldn't stand still. The general curiosity slowly swung to him.

'There's to be a new Foreman.'

The platers were sceptical. 'Wish there was!' 'Where d'you buy that, then?'

'Eric Strachey, who else?'

Trigg laughed, 'Well, that's a right rag and bone shop. What's Strachey know about it?'

'Ah, well, it seems you don't know everything, 'Lias. 'Cause Eric Strachey's got a fancy lady. You didn't know that, did you?'

'I call it a funny fancy, if she's got him. The mind boggles. Who is it, then?'

'What! It's Mrs Bagnold.'

'Well, that's a Jack Sprat and his wife. Anyway, so what? Mrs Bagnold is a big issue, but she isn't Stacey, is she?'

'Yes, well, you really are a poor ignorant sod, 'Lias. 'Cause she works in the office next to Strudwick's, and those partition walls are thin, see, and what do you think she heard this morning?'

'I'm damned if I know. Do you know, Vic?'

'No, 'Lias, I ain't heard. But then, you see, I ain't a good-looking Don Gee-o-varney, not like Eric Strachey.'

'Nah, mate, that's tough on you. 'Course, young Eric now, he's what you'd call a Ro-meo, i'n'e Nutty? He's a Liberace!'

'A Liberace, 'Lias? Don't you mean a Casanova?'

'Dunno, Nutty. I seen it on the telly.'

'And it was good! It was very good, 'Lias'

'D'you see it, Vic?'

'I saw it, 'Lias, I thought it was lousy. It was all about bloody Eye-ties!'

'It was, Victor, yes, that was their mistake. They should have had Eric Strachey. Yes, Reginald! You were saying?'

Barrett shouted, 'I was saying, blast you, that Mrs Bagnold heard Strudwick and Forbes thrash it all out between them, this morning. Who'll be Foreman, and that. It's all tied up.'

The platers stared at him: the idea couldn't take hold. Barrett was pent-up in disappointment. 'Oh bleeding hell, don't you want to know who it is?'

The platers slowly looked round to Jim Dawson, who stood tense, quiet, very white.

Barrett was frenzied with impatience now, he blurted, 'It isn't Jim!'

The platers all stared at him: at last he had them. He paused, then sang out, 'It's Edgar Warboys!' That took the wind from everyone's sails. The platers, grave, avoided looking at Dawson, who stood with his face down. Eventually, Trigg said, 'God, Clyde'll be pleased, that'll make his day! It breaks my arse, and all.'

Barrett, exasperated, flung now into indignation. 'What's wrong with Edgar Warboys, then? He's been a charge-hand ever so long!'

'Not long enough,' a plater said. 'What's wrong with Jim?'

'Search me,' Barrett shouted. 'I only know what Eric Strachey told me, confidential. But I have heard it said, the thing about Jim is, he's too good a plater to take off the floor.'

At this, the platers did all turn to Dawson. The unfairness stunned them, and they could only look at him with one grimness of sympathy, while a general murmur raggedly shaped to the words, 'It's a shame.' Dawson clamped his mouth in tighter compression.

'Here comes his blooming majesty,' Trigg said: Warboys himself was swinging their way. He did not know that they knew, but there was a spring in his step, he did not feel the heat, a smile that he could not keep back crinkled the corners of his mouth, and danced in his eyes.

'Is he still in there?' he asked, nodding towards the hatch. Though indeed he still meant to be the sometime equal and good old mate, a new edge hardened on his voice involuntarily. He heard it himself, and the others all heard it.

The platers folded their arms, and watched with dour

faces that gave nothing away.

Barrett, to show Warboys to good advantage, publicly asked him, 'Er, Edgar, what do you think we ought to do?'

'Lias Trigg promptly looked at Dawson, and said, 'Er, James, what, in your opinion, do you reckon we should do?' Warboys took note of that. He would give Trigg something to laugh about in due course. For the present, he spoke out:

'I say, something should be done about this. Think of all the money gone to pot, while we're just sitting here. Where is Clyde? Where has the blasted man got to?'

Dawson said, 'We'd best wait till Petchey opens up.' He made it clear in his voice, he wanted no remarks on his passing over.

The platers nodded: the stagnant heat was intense, the sweat forked and converged and streamed down their faces. Warboys reflected, then took full responsibility, announcing:

'Well, we'd better get on, anyway. We'd better find other jobs to do. Let's get moving, then.'

He spoke with force, but all that happened was that 'Lias Trigg put up his hand, like a boy in school,

'Er, Mr Warboys. Point of order, Mr Warboys.'

Warboys turned on Trigg half-closed glimmering eyes of misgiving.

'Mr Warboys, sir, I'm sorry, but I got a better idea than that. I think what we ought to do, in the present situation, is, go down the Marina, and have a dip.'

'The Marina, 'Lias?!' Saville exclaimed.

Watts heaved himself to his feet. ''Lias, I think you're right.'

The other platers looked round the shop. Half of them were off work, there was no Clyde, no Strudwick, the place was neglected. And the untoward idea caught, the rest of them got up.

'Hey, come back, where are you off to?' Warboys demanded.

But the coast was clear, and the men walked away, other men, at their benches, catching on and joining in. At an easy pace the growing crowd trooped out at the far end of the shop.

Barrett fluttered about Warboys, pulling his cigarette to shreds. 'What you gona do, Edgar, what you gona do about it?'

'By Christ, I'll fetch you one, if you don't let me think,' Warboys muttered, sitting down on a vacated toolbox. The gilt was off the gingerbread: truly, he thought, no one loves a man in a position of responsibility. Trigg would pay for this.

35

The flood of platers surged through the Steel Stores, breached the ramshackle fencing, and climbed the railway embankment at the bottom of the works. They picked their way between the lines, and stood for a moment spread out along the track, gazing down at the flooded pits and abandoned machinery of the old sand-works. There was no breeze, and the willows round the lakes were as motionless as the rusty engines and overturned trucks. The men scrambled and skidded to the bottom, and stripped off where they stood. The sun burned their indoor skin; Surtees the blacksmith tested the water with one sensitive toe; while Trigg, who had brought them there, raced across the grass and burst into the water with a vast concussion and splash.

The platers swam out in all directions. Patrick Collier stood on the edge, enjoying the contrast of the scorching sun on his skin and the cold thought of the water. Then he found that, as a man due to be married, he was an object of inspection to the other platers. He launched himself in a clear arc: he slid through splash, there was a shock of coolness and bubbling perturbation, and then he was underwater, swimming in slow strokes through the delicious cold, high over the fogged khaki depths. He surfaced in exploding spray, and worked his way across the pool on his back, till an oily hand, water standing on it in tight beads, swung down into his face and he went under again. He came up choking and hurling streams into the puckered and dripping faces of Trigg and Tony Wilmot, who surged and frolicked like shaved walruses through the sparkling and jumping scuds of splash. Then Wilmot wheeled his long arms backwards and rode away, almost sitting up in his bow-wave, his long clean pink body and large rib-cage displayed. 'Lias Trigg slowly heeled over, till the white whale-hump of his stomach rocked above the waters, which took rainbow colours from the dissolving oil.

The thinning oil on Rob Sleath's skin helped the water to run into his eyes and sting. But the delight, just to dawdle, treading water, to ease acid aching shoulders in the cool, and to dip tired feet, that had stifled in heavy boots all day, into the chilly waters lower down.

The apprentices raced in the deeps, while the older platers paddled in the shallows. There were revelations, as when Jimmy Marlow, who always wore his long auburn hair brushed round in a sleek disc over his brow, surfaced with a bald head they had not seen before, and streaming auburn-to-black locks hanging down one side of his head to his shoulders. The platers studied also the whole revealed body of Perce Bowditch, the slow plater. He was not so slow as to miss the swim, but still he was a prodigy, for while most of the platers had white or pink bodies, with only their forearms and faces dark, it seemed that all the oil of all the machinery, all the scarf and filings of iron, all the rough muck and tat in the shop, had sailed with ease through any clothing Bowditch ever wore, so he appeared before them one dark blurr of oily grime. Most of the platers scrubbed every atom of the shop off them as soon as they got home, and they gazed in wonder at—they had never beheld—such a dirty man. Bowditch was not offended, he took it lightly and made a performance of sluicing water over his face and hands. He was aggrieved only when a grim taciturn plater called Maurice Strether, who was a Jehovah's Witness, waded into the shallows, looked at him with disapproval, then, to the surprise of all of them, started singing at the top of his voice, 'I will wash you—whiter than snow—'

The finer singing was provided by Wilmot, who stood in the middle depths, with water up to his heaving chest and his head thrown back, and gave them as seldom before the chorus from *La Boheme*. Some of the platers now sprawled in the sun. Victor Watts sat up, nursing with great precaution a slight gash he had caught under the water. Others were propped on their elbows, watching where, while the depths of the pit were unfathomable and cold, all over its sunlit surface there were splashes and kicking legs and flying arms and bursts of fresh spray.

36

To Clyde's surprise the door of the Time Study Office was open. At his tentative push it swung wide, and showed the office deserted. Time-sheets, job-cards and new blue-white ammonia-prints lolled across tea-cups and wire trays. Biros and stopwatches were left here and there, and a well-chewed pipe of Bert Cherry's smouldered in the ashtray.

Clyde came in stealthily, conscious of the muffled clink of his iron and the low creaking of his boots. He took in with contempt the out-of-date calendars, and Bert Cherry's doodlings on the partition wall. The next door would be Forbes's: he went across and tapped on it, hollow with nerves.

There was no answer. He tapped again and just caught a subdued and unwilling 'Who is it?'

Clyde opened the door anyway, saying hoarsely as he walked in, 'You'll know why I've come to see you, Mr Forbes.'

Forbes, whom Clyde normally thought of as a sharp brisk mechanism of aluminium, simply leaned back in his chair with a weary shrug, and dully registered Clyde. He did not seem surprised or embarrassed by the visit, though Clyde towered over him enraged, hulking, his face inflamed, a fierce unsteady dance in his eyes.

Perplexed, restraining himself, Clyde asked, 'It's true, then?'

Forbes looked at him, then looked round his office, then looked at him again, and nodded and sighed together.

Clyde's throat clogged. 'Could you tell me, Mr Forbes, who it's to be?'

Forbes slowly frowned. 'Who's to be what?'

It was too much, Clyde's jacket clanged, he struck the table with his fist and cried, 'Oh by the Lord Harry, will you tell me who's taking over the Plate Shop after me?'

Forbes blinked; then, with a brief revival of his briskness, he said, 'What are you talking about?'

'Oh my godfathers,' Clyde moaned, he was in real pain. 'Will you just tell me, Mr Forbes, please—is it true, or isn't it, that I've been sacked from the Plate Shop?'

'Yes, oh yes.' Forbes nodded in a weary singsong.

With this said, Clyde recovered firmness. 'Well, I should like an explanation, please.'

Forbes looked at him quizzically. 'You're not the only one, you know.'

Clyde shouted, 'What are we at, Mr Forbes?'

'Good God, doesn't everyone in the place know by now? We've heard from Crowley.'

'Heard from Crowley?' Now it was Clyde who could not connect with Forbes's thought.

'Yes, that's it, he's made up his mind. He's come to his conclusions.' Forbes got up. 'Edward, I've been sitting here hours, I need some air.' He said no more, but led the way out.

*

They came out into the sunlight from the huddle of offices built lean-to against the Plate Shop. This courtyard was the centre of the factory. The workshops looked into it over the heads of the offices. On one side ran the Drawing Office, brilliantly lit, with the white-shirted men at their slanted boards tiny and sharp-edged as in a slide held up to the light. Across the yard was the square plain blue shape of the Machine Shop, and the brown hump of the foundry, rising out of its brown scrap-heaps and stockpiles of castings like a large creature half-buried and straining clear. The two blast-furnaces, with their plated shoulders and slanted hoods, stood over the yard like watching giants. All the works pressed round this yard, and waited: though all it had in it, over to one side, bare, shut-up, turning the eye back with its smoky-silvery reflections, was the caravan.

Between the Machine Shop and the foundry a long tarmac avenue sloped away between lesser shops, silos and stores. The two men walked over to this avenue, while Forbes told Clyde musingly, 'Crowley's got through the profit and the loss, now. He's worked out, there are two departments here that make a clear profit. You'll want to know what they are. Well, they're the plaster-mixers, and the drills division.'

'Plaster!' Clyde scoffed. 'And the others?'

Forbes looked at him with a muted quizzical pity. The others? Ah well.'

'We sell all we make. Dammit, I know we do!'

'Yes, but it's complicated, Edward. The long and the short of it is, he's got our custom now. And he's got Exells. They make what we make, and, after all, they could sell more than they do. So you see, what he'll do now, is to slap our label on their machines, and then—flog them off.'

'Well, well, what'll he do to us?'

They paused between the tall red columns of the castings, and the corrugated blue wall of the Machine Shop. It rose beside them in an iron cliff, muffling the whine of lathes and drills.

'Well, he has a section out of town, doesn't he? He's going to expand that, and our Waterfind Division goes out there. He'll take on the machinery, and the men.'

'They're leaving the site?'

Forbes smiled agedly at Clyde's feeling on this point. 'Oh yes, they're leaving the site. And on the other hand, he's going to put up a new workshop here, where the foundry is —that's to make plaster mixers properly.'

Clyde gazed up at the rusty towers of the blast-furnaces. 'What'll happen to the foundry?'

'Well, that'll come down. He needs the space for the new shop.'

'And the Paint Shops?'

'They'll come down.'

'And the Metal Stores; and the Machine Shop?'

'They're coming down. He can get money for the machinery, you see. And some of the space he'll use for warehousing. The rest of it, and the yard the other side of you, all that, he'll sell as land. You've no idea the price of land. Well, of course, it isn't always easy to get planning permission to do that. But, Edward, he done it.' Forbes smiled again the quick tired smile—it came and went in a moment—which seemed the only way he had of shaping his feelings.

The whole ironclad mass of Clyde was weak and lost. There was a dazzled turmoil in his head where men swarmed like ants over the roofs of the workshops, breaking them up so that the panels streamed down like leaves, and the exposed iron ribs stood jagged, then folded in. Balls on chains swung into crumbling breakages of concrete skewered with buckled iron. Everything levelled down to a concrete plain which itself was shattered by pneumatic drills and scraped and bulldozed away leaving nothing, except that through all the ruin the silvery caravan sat there unchanged. He saw this. But he also saw clearly in his mind, as something too enormous to be vulnerable, what also faced him in the real world when he turned back and saw, across the yard, rising over the jumbled conglomeration of offices piled against its untiring walls: grey, scarred, immemorially solid: the enormous long mountain bulk of his own shop. So he asked:

'What about the Plate Shop?'

'Oh, that'll come down.'

'And my platers?'

'Some of them he'll take to Exells. It can't be many, of course. One or two may go into plaster mixers. The rest will be—where we will be.'

Clyde had no words.

*

They had come, at the end of the avenue, to the place where everyone went, when they wanted to get away and smoke quietly, the Dump. It was an iron wilderness. There were tumbled piles of spare guards and cowlings; mounds of defective engines; and the great irregular crush of un-sold, damaged or abandoned machines. Ancient mixers that Clyde hadn't seen for years stood with their intricate tackle all exposed and their quaint hoods sharp against the sky. They were as beautiful in his eyes as old works of art. In those days the machines were coloured a pale milky azure, but the soft blue was dusted and pitted all over with corrosion, as though the iron had diseased blood. Beyond were relics of still older machines that were just one eruption of burning rust. They were so brittle a finger could snap off the metal in flakes, leaving razor-edged tears like claw-marks. All the iron in the yard, the whole steel acreage, was slowly incinerating in the atmosphere, and here the oldest embers finally crumbled and melted down to a red ash of consumed metal.

The iron was everywhere hot to the touch, and the breezeless staling air throbbed with heat so that the broken, corroded shapes rippled and trembled as if they were seen through the invisible fire that was everywhere at work, or even through running water. But of water, of moisture, there was nowhere a drop, bar the odd tepid pool that collected in a mixer-bowl, with a brown skin or scum thick upon it, water that not only corroded the iron but was itself corroding.

In this maze of burning iron, where part was, what all of it was like, the smouldering rakings and clinkers brought up from the foundry, they sauntered, and sat down in the shade. They were surprised by a fellow-feeling, but this was so big a departure that they hardly knew what to do. As a token, they swapped cigarettes. But presently Forbes was again aware of a distance growing between them. For some time Clyde had returned nothing to his own stray remarks, he only sat, in the sweltering shade of a large disused plant, heaving long shuddering breaths. He looked so little himself that Forbes wondered if the shock had given him a heart attack.

Clyde couldn't talk any more, for in his mind a further knowledge was slowly collecting, till he murmured, 'It's a judgement on me.'

'Edward . . .' Forbes began, but Clyde looked at him and said with emphasis, 'I'm to blame for this.' The past years had all come clear as glass, and all he could see, looking back, was his long fight to keep the Time Study, Forbes, his own men, the new machinery, at bay; only he knew how much hindering and obstruction he had done. Now suddenly it was all laid clear to his view, as by a bomb-blast. He could see nothing else.

'It isn't your fault, Edward,' Forbes tried to say, soothingly. It was clear to him that the loss was no more Clyde's fault, than it was anyone else's: it was too big to be the fault of one man only. But Clyde, looking at him, scarcely heard him and didn't believe him. His heart was breaking, and Forbes could only wonder at the strange crossed routes of Clyde's conscience and his conceit that made him want, where surely there was already enough real cause for grief and reproach, to embrace not only that, but also to heap on himself, like the man on the cross, the blame for everything.

37

Some of the platers, wanting to make a discreet return to the Plate Shop, came up the narrow passage between the Machine Shop and the Stores. They reckoned to stroll down the avenue from the Dump, in the guise of men worn out by lugging a new batch of mixers to be painted. They soon regretted it, for the passage had a floor of old piping and angle-iron. They had to climb up at the end, to get on to the avenue, and the first man was barely out, when he ducked back in again, and the whole queue concertinaed, hemmed in by two walls of workshop as though they were caught in a gigantic press. Across the thin strip of light at the end, the large slow mass of Clyde stalked past: set over them on the avenue, he cut out the light like a door. They peered out after him, and watched his square back moving deliberately across the sunlit yard towards his shop. The platers at the front climbed out and walked down after him, those at the back reversed, and behind the Paint Shops they flitted and dodged stealthily like his familiar spirits.

He was standing in the middle of the shop, looking only vaguely puzzled to find it empty, when the two lots of platers advanced on him from different ends, so that now he was trapped in a large living press. They slowed as they approached, and he hardly needed to speak. Hawkins asked, 'What's happened, Mr Clyde?'

He spoke quietly, as though an important part of him had failed. 'We're all sold up. Crowley's done his sums now. The shop is coming down.'

There was no more to say. He left them, and clambered up the stairs to his office, making a broad stooping silhouette in the entrance before the door closed and he was gone.

Jimmy Marlow, still braced and keen from his swimming, muttered weakly, 'The old fool's off his rocker.'

The platers besieged Hawkins, who could only say, 'Steady on, slow down, he's got it wrong for sure. The union hasn't heard anything about this. And we'd be the first to know.' He dismissed the possibility. Then he, Marlow and Riley drew apart in urgent talk, while more platers, damp but sunny, came in over the embankment, and the consternation spread.

Presently Josh came down from the office, and like a stout spool he wound the anxious men round him. But he told them no more than Clyde had. Crowley was closing the shop and they were all finished. His face still wore its wide smile, though his glasses had misted white and were like frozen pools in a bank of red earth.

Fire from heaven descended on Reg Barrett, he cried in inspiration, 'Eric Strachey's the man! Eric Strachey'll know about it!' Hawkins pitied him, but none the less the platers peeled off from Josh and thickened in a larger knot that had at its centre Eric Strachey, pretty cool and dry considering, and clear that nothing took place in the works that he didn't know about. When the others went swimming he stole away to Mrs Bagnold, and he found himself in a position to inform them that, yes, actually the Plate Shop was coming down, and not just the Plate Shop, but the Foundry, the Machine Shop, the Paint Shop and the Offices, in short the whole works. It was putting it mildly to say that half of them would be laid off because in fact all of them would be on the streets, and as to whether it was true that there wasn't the money available to pay their redundancy, yes it was true, the till was empty and they were already working free and gratis. But Eric Strachey knew too much for his own good. He was jeered at, jostled, abused. He bore it pretty well: his cigarette wagged nonchalently stuck to his bottom lip, he spat from time to time, and occasionally came in raucous and righteous in support of his jeremiads.

His details they dismissed, but the men left him slowly, seriously troubled. They cast round for anyone who might know more. The Time Study was supposed to be thick as thieves with management, and now the currents crossed and snagged, and eddied round one or another dazed time-studier, as man by man they were brought to light. But the young ones were gormless, they had no idea. Ted the Australian was ironic and pessimistic, they agreed with him but learned little. Bert Cherry puffed his pipe like a bonfire of damp cow-parsley, and went round in circles, but from him they learned nothing.

Warboys shouted, 'This won't do! We can't have this!' in a high voice of personal affront, as if he thought the catastrophe had been expressly engineered to do him out of being Foreman. He upbraided the union men, but they were as shocked, angry and anxious as everyone else. Hawkins announced that he, Riley and Marlow would go and see management right away; and the three of them set off. The others were supposed to wait till they got back. But the platers were unattached anyway, and it happened inevitably that as Hawkins, Riley and Marlow walked out of the shop, the platers' anxious leaning after them turned into a flow. They caught up the three men, and tramped with them into the yard.

The Production Controller, Forbes, was their first port of call. They crowded into the Time Study Office, and banged on his door.

Forbes had only just got back to his office, and was by no means ready to meet an army. He felt as though a heavy breaker burst on him, when he opened the door, and saw the office beyond crowded back to the corridor with impatient faces. There were so many men, he was overwhelmed and couldn't place them.

As soon as the platers saw his pale worried face, and his eyes flickering behind his sharp glasses, the whole crowd moved forward. To Forbes they looked like a lynch-mob: and as they saw his alarm they all started speaking, in the grip of a hatred they scarcely knew they had,

'Wup there, machine-man.'

'Stuff you, Forbs-ee.'

'Give him oil, Nutty, the poor bugger's running dry.'

'It was news to me,' Forbes said loudly. The platers only hooted. Eventually he moved back, and Hawkins, Riley, and as many other men as could find room, crowded into Forbes's office. Forbes got behind his desk, and started explaining, but there was constant movement and interruption, neither he nor his audience were clear what he was saying.

Then Strudwick arrived, and unlike Forbes he attacked on sight. 'Here, what the devil's all this?' he shouted, and promptly muscled in. 'Ee, you buggers, let me through, will you?' He pushed through, regardless of the unwilling lock of close-packed men. No one wished him ill, and yet he came out the other side flushed, his brilliant shirt crumpled and hanging out, his tie at half-mast. He hastily and discreetly repaired the damage as he joined Forbes behind his desk, and took over. He agreed, they would have a meeting now, he'd invite all the Stewards in the works, he'd get Stacey to come, and everything that management knew, the men would know. He himself had only just heard; he was in the same boat. That said, he cleared the room. He had agreed that half a dozen men from the Plate Shop could come in, provided that they came in the character of a Committee.

Outside the offices, Hawkins explained. Riley and Marlow were on the committee of course; two places might go for lesser unions. George Reynolds and Jim Dawson also found themselves on the committee, not for any office they held, and not at all by Hawkins' wish, but because the whole movement of the men simply forced them to the front, and forcibly stood them where the committee stood. The hastily got-up committee went back into the office.

The meeting was now all ready, except that no one had seen Stacey go in. It was suspected that quiet back ways had been used to effect, they had smuggled him through and he lay in wait within.

Presently there was a jostling at the back of the crowd, and a gap opened in it. Some way beyond stood the tall dark-suited column of Stacey.

He was blowing his nose. As silence fell, he raised his eyes from his handkerchief and gave the men a long emotionless stare. Then he straightened abruptly, gave a quick final sniff, and started forward: about his nose there clung the slight contraction of a sniff. A way opened for him. The men stepped back and without embarrassment or visible interest he walked slowly into the office.

38

The platers stood around in the yard, chatting in nervous
starts. In spite of the warning on the works petrol pump
behind them, they smoked as though they wanted nothing so
much as to go up in flames. They bunched quickly: a door
had opened, there was a glimpse of men talking. Then the
Stewards and the others trooped out, with faces so contained
and grave that no one needed to ask what the meeting's
upshot was.

The men from all the shops in the factory walked round
to the large yard the other side of the Plate Shop. There the
Stewards climbed onto the trailer of a lorry, and what scarcely
needed announcing, was announced. Not only they, but
management also, were scrapped. Half the board was already
voted off, and Stacey was replaced by a managing director
from Mackworth Crowley. A works manager from Exells
would replace Strudwick. Forbes's department would be run
down forthwith, Mackworth Crowley had newer methods.
There was a cheer at this, it was the one consolation to find
that even the Time Study was demolished by time. For the
men themselves the situation was worse even than they had
thought. Very few men would stay on, and the plaster mixers
and drills would mainly be made by men from Exells. As to

finding work elsewhere—they knew what the chances were, these days. And as to retraining schemes, the local ones were full just now, but the men could put their names down if they liked. There would be some money from Mackworth Crowley for redundancy, retraining, and pensions.

Chapter and verse convinced, and one man's repeated cry, 'I don't believe it!' registered only the shock of having to believe this. As to what should be done, the breath was too much knocked out of all of them for there to be any plan yet. Of course, all these matters would go to union head offices today: the Stewards were emphatic. But no one was hopeful, and the general complaint turned to a shared, flat, 'That's that, then. A sell-out,' when they heard that Crowley, as he claimed, was already negotiating the shutdown with the unions. Probably it was true: he owned many factories, and the unions sometimes let things go at one factory to win a raise at another. They all knew, Crowley was someone with whom the unions did a lot of negotiating, in London.

On one side of the crowd an argument started, centering on Jim Bundy. While he insisted, the other men took sides, till he found he was making a speech. His loose khaki shirt flapped as he waved his arms vaguely; through a grey stain of oil half washed off, his eyes were biting, and his harsh voice seemed to hit his words into the men's heads with a hammer:

'They say it makes a loss, do they? Well, if it makes a loss, we know why. They haven't the shit of an idea how to run the place. They get old *Forbsy*, he puts in a *Time Study*, well, who works faster for that? And it makes bad blood. And we can twist the buggers round our fingers. Then they get *Strudwick*, and what does *Strudwick* do? Well, he comes up the ground, he kicks the ball about a bit with common sods like us, and he does marvels for the team—we only lose half the matches now. That's what *Strudwick* does—that, and buying new suits in *Burtons*. Any fucking one of us could run the place better—and that's what I say. Why don't we get it sorted out, so we keep it going? If *Crowley* comes up here—kick the bugger out, and park his caravan on top of him! We'd do a bloody sight better on our own.'

He was quiet normally, he spoke strongly now. But at the end Hawkins was sceptical, he wasn't sure what the union would think; and most of the listening faces were stirred, but full of doubt.

'It wouldn't work, Jim,' said Victor Watts.

'Nah, it wouldn't work.' 'It wouldn't work,' murmured the stolid sceptical English faces.

That was all they said. The idea fluttered through the crowd like a mauled bird on broken wings, and didn't get off the dusty concrete.

*

Warboys walked up to Hawkins, and shouted at him as though he wanted to knock him over, 'I want to know—what is going to happen to the charge-hands? I've a right to know that! Who's being kicked out, and who's being kept on?'

Hawkins was the general butt, the other platers were shouting at him all at once, 'You let us in for this, Hawkins.' 'It's your fault, Hawkins.' 'Union won't do anything, you know that, don't you, Hawkins?' To all this Hawkins nodded, and gazed through the shouting men. He had another worry now. He had used union money to paint his house, and there was no way he could get the money back, before the men found out about it. And what could he say? He borrowed money like this every year, and he always put it back. Everyone did it, but he couldn't say that. He didn't feel guilty now, but he knew that when it all came out, and they were all looking at him, he would feel like filth. And now was his hour: he could strangle Crowley, his passion was all on fire, it was the chance for him to do something in the union, after all the piddling rubbish of day-to-day business—Barrett and his little ends, Pethick, and so on. It was such a pity, such a wicked shame, now all his best feelings were ready, that they should all be spoilt and dirtied by this fly in the ointment. The men wanted to knife him already, they would kill him when they found out about the money. There was nothing he could do to prevent it, and in the meantime for hours or even a day he had to hurry on the union business, as if nothing were wrong. He was the one who had to start the wheels moving, which in due course would break him up.

He squared himself, and said to Marlow, 'Jim boy, we'd better have a Stewards' meeting, soon as we can. Let's use the canteen. We'd better have old Reynolds along, an old hand, knows it all. I don't look forward to that.'

He scratched his pale scalp; what other things did he have to do?

*

'What a fucking great start to a marriage!' Patrick Collier said. He saw Wally Reed, Pethick's friend, standing next to him, and said, 'So we're all off down Pethick's road, then.' But Reed only looked dazed. He hardly knew what to feel. He had worked there all his life, but he didn't care for the boring work he did. He had always said he did it for the money, and the firm could go hang. None the less, half his life had gone into the works, and now the first shock was over, he was pulled different ways, he could get nothing clear.

The platers rallied George Reynolds, '*You're* all right,

George. You've only got a month to go till you get your pension, haven't you?'

Reynolds echoed what they said, 'I can't complain—got my pension coming next month, any road.' His face and voice cracked in a dead chuckle, he looked not less but more shattered than the younger men.

Behind him Strether, the Jehovah's Witness, stood with his head bowed and his eyes closed. The thought that he might be praying kept everyone clear of him.

Several men went at Jim Dawson. 'Ah, Jim *you'll* get fixed up, *you* won't want for work.' Dawson was so skilled, it was impossible that he wouldn't get work; but he wouldn't admit it, he insisted he was as anxious as everyone else. The platers stayed near him, as if his skill were a talisman.

Victor Watts, looking on, kept asking, 'What are *we* going to do, for Christ's sake?' His voice sang high, he looked ready to weep; 'Lias Trigg, disapproving, gave him a great clap on the back that nearly sent him flying, and shouted in his ear, 'Hit the road, Jack!'

'Lias, I'll slaughter you.'

'Slaughter 'Lias? !' Nutty Saville exclaimed.

They turned to Eric Strachey, who had said nothing so far. He had ceased to know more than anyone else, and was left to his last dryness. They asked him, 'Here, Eric, are you pretty cut up about this?' He paused, reflected, and then said, 'No, I'm not sorry about this.' Then they asked him, 'Well, Eric, are you glad about it?' He thought a little and said, 'No, I'm not glad about it.' They left him to his devices.

One of the time-studiers, the Australian, Ted, had come to the meeting. He had been a welder for years, and he had come by instinct. The platers were pleased to see him. 'Time's up then, Ted.' 'Well, Ted, will you time us on the dole-queue ?'

'What'll you stop-watch now, Ted?' They expected something from him so dry and sharp, it would cut them like a cheese-wire, but he let them down: he was silenced.

Later, when they kept on, he cocked an eye and said, 'I'll be OK, don't you worry, matey. I'll see to it that I'm all right. I look after Number One, that's for sure.' He insisted on it, as though he were the world's wonder of self-interest.

The men most out in the cold were those like Perce Bowditch, who had worked in the factory all their lives and never been much good. The firm had carried them, and they had nothing else. Bowditch had only ten years to go, he would never get another job. He gazed about him mute, cut-off from everyone else. Then, as he stood hitching his trousers or scratching the seamed back of his neck, he started saying to whoever came near him, 'I don't know what I'll do.' His pale eyes were wide and at sea, he said again, 'I don't know what I'll do.'

The men were scattered now in small groups and knots, dotted across the concrete. They had stopped talking about the firm, and when they did come back to it, some said they were sold out by the union, some by Stacey, some by Strudwick. Some said it had to come, they had been losing money for years; some said that all in all they weren't losing money, and the order-books were full. The simple emotion they had felt earlier, about what had happened and the rights and wrongs of it, had dispersed; and to some of the men it seemed strange and sad, that they were passing together through the greatest crisis in the factory's life, and no two of them could agree on what it meant.

39

Strudwick was looking for something. Under Forbes's amazed eyes, he opened one after another of Forbes's cupboards until he ferreted out, among the stationery, a dusty bottle of sherry and three glasses upended on an aluminium tray.

'I thought I'd get there, Ray,' he said. 'Dammit, man, we need this!' The tray floated through the office to the desk, and he poured out for all three. Stacey sat back, one long collapse, in Forbes's chair. Forbes half-sat on the desk-top, hugging himself, drawn tight in preoccupation. But Strudwick, as he handed round the sherry, looked more and more as though he had already drunk it. At the sight of it alone he flushed, his eyes sparkled, his face swelled.

'Oh, did we need this!' he said, it was his nearest approach to a toast; and evidently he did need it for he downed the glass in one and poured another. Forbes took the glass he was offered and sipped from it at regular intervals, unawares. Stacey gazed at his, left on the desk where Strudwick put it, in a kind of paralysed hunger as though, but for the invisible threads that tied him everywhere, he would sit forward and eat glass and all.

Thus repaired, Strudwick instinctively—it was the nature of the man—bustled about Forbes's room, re-arranging the chairs and restoring all things to their original order. 'I like to leave things as I find them,' he said.

In all this, Forbes smelt a rat. 'Carl, have you thought what you might do afterwards?'

Strudwick looked up, and his eye was caught by Forbes's. 'Ee, Ray, you'll cut yourself It's true, though. I did a bit of phoning. Of course, it's a small firm, but there—a General Manager was what they asked for. And beggers can't be choosers!'

Forbes stared at him, almost awed. He thought, 'I couldn't do that.'

Strudwick saw Forbes didn't approve. He glanced at Stacey, but Stacey hadn't listened. He added, 'No, Ray, no, I'd been wanting to move, it was time for a change. And I'd kept my eyes open, since Crowley hove in sight—be stupid not to. I expect you did, eh? Eh?'

Forbes sighed, he had had quite other thoughts.

Strudwick chased the sherry with a deep draught of air. 'Dammit, I'm tired after all that jaw! But what a man Crowley is, eh?'

'I wasn't struck.'

'Oh, Ray, haven't you seen how his shares have done? You have to give it to the man!' He burst out exultant. 'Companies like that will rule the world!'

Forbes quietly said, 'Perhaps you should have tried to stay on, Carl? Get a foot on the ladder.'

'Dammit, perhaps I should,' Strudwick said seriously; but nothing could keep him down for long. 'No, no, I've made my move.' His eyes brightened, he rocked on his feet, he was evidently soaring in some high balloon, thinking what a thing it was, to be a General Manager.

Forbes resumed his desultory exchange with Stacey,

which, as with Clyde, had an equality in disinheritance that they hadn't known before.

'I'm still not clear just *where* we were losing,' Forbes said, 'I go over and over it, and I don't see it.'

'No, Ray,' Stacey murmured, 'The plants lost money.'

'I know they weren't in the black yet.'

'Oh no, Ray, they lost money.'

In spite of the sherry, Strudwick showed traces of depression and moved over to the window. He looked out, 'Dammit, the buggers have all cleared off!'

The waxy lids of Stacey's eyes turned again to Forbes. He said, 'I blame myself for this.' Then he sat forward, and slowly turned his glass of sherry round on the desk-top. 'I don't know, Ray. They say we lost money, but . . .' he trailed off. But presently he pulled himself out of his chair, and towered up lean and tall like a grieving stork. 'You see, it isn't clear to me that all in all we made a loss. Well, it depends how you look at it. You can do a lot with accounts; and I don't question Crowley's maths. He's good at sums, Crowley, he'll make money all right. D'you know, Ray, when he was here, he priced everything. There isn't a nut or a bolt, but he knows what it'll fetch. But still, however you work it out, it's clear to me that he'd make a darn sight more money in the long run, if he keeps us going. Oh yes. But for that, instead of taking money out, he'd have to put money in.'

Here Stacey laughed, and stopped; then both men were solemn. They had a tragic respect for the principle of profit: a firm might be good, but if it made a loss, it should go to the wall. When he first tried to come to terms with the crash, Forbes did at least know that he was meeting: necessity. But to find, after all, that it wasn't even this harsh law that had done for them, but only the principle of a quicker sort of profit, a quick killing—it left Forbes helpless with fury.

Stacey's mouth crinkled. 'You know, Ray, it's enough to make me vote'—he laughed—'liberal.' His shoulders settled into the usual round stoop, from which burdens slid. 'Ah well, don't let it eat you. What's it matter, in the end? You think that wheels have to be kept turning, don't you? Probably you think it all leads somewhere. I don't think it leads anywhere. Leave it, Ray.'

Stacey spoke in an unusual, kindly voice, but if Forbes was going to join him one day, he hadn't got there yet. He couldn't slide out of his useless, profitless fury with Crowley. The years of work he had put into the factory, so very much was tied up in it—the Crowleys ran round in their big circle trampling everyone, and they all went hell-for-leather because they would fall if they didn't run faster all the time to keep up, and faster and faster the circle went, where would it end?

Stacey stood by the window, and the sherry occasionally, mechanically, moved to his lips.

Even Strudwick was dampened and reflective. He was thinking, he liked to move, but each new move they made was harder for his wife. She didn't uproot and dig in again easily, as he did.

But, it had to be; and the new job was a good one; and he couldn't pretend he wasn't excited. The young man in him rekindled, at the prospect of the open road, and the wide world for his oyster. He decided that he didn't need, but none the less would give himself, another glass of Forbes's sherry.

40

Barry tapped on the door of the narrow, slightly curving house, then stepped back. The windows were black, there was no sign of life; the yellow-black bricks had a brittle hardened skin, like a rind, flaking away. A few flowers fought upwards in the ragged strip of garden, almost colourless under a powdery veil of dust.

The small window of coloured glass brightened as though a candle had been lit on the other side, and he made out, moving from side to side across the light, a growing bright shape, now red, now blue, now amber, that determined into a face.

The door opened and Ewa Pethick looked out. 'Oh. Barry.' Her voice was simply cold and hard, it surprised him like a knock from a piece of iron.

'Ewa, can I come in?'

Her open cold eyes said, Why?

'I want to see your dad. I've some news . . .'

She gave him a quick clear look that dulled into misgiving. Then she let him in and led the way to the kitchen, where the Pethicks sat round the small table, scarcely touching their tea. She reminded her parents who Barry was, and Mrs Pethick's square tight-jawed face sharpened and pointed at him. Pethick himself nodded absently: the rippling and crumpled lines of good-humour still survived in his face, but his eyes were dim and peering, an old man's eyes, as though he were looking through them from a cold place far inside himself.

Mrs Pethick brought a chair to the table. 'Sit down, Mr Spurrier.'

He sat; she sat; Ewa sat. Mrs Pethick, blinking rapidly at the teapot as though she were giving it some sharp slaps, poured Barry some tea. No one spoke, and Barry realized that though he sat at table with them, the three made a tight closed ring and he was outside it. He was as separate from them, as if he were not in the room at all. Obviously they were silent because they were waiting for him to say whatever he had come to say, before he went away.

'I wanted to tell you,' he began, but his voice sounded to him like someone else speaking badly in public, 'why it was that no one could do anything, to put things right, after the way Clyde treated you. The reason is, Crowley has made his mind up now, about what he wants to do with the works—'

At the mention of the works, Pethick's eyes went down to his plate; but as to the decision, he had no curiosity.

'He's scrapping the place. The Plate Shop's coming down, the men are all laid off, Clyde's out.'

Pethick nodded, but at the same time he looked blankly at Barry, and seemed to ask, with the slight shrug he gave, 'So? What's that to me?'

Ewa looked at Barry intensely, but he could not tell what the intense stare meant.

Barry ran aground, he had only confused ideas about why he had come. He felt he must stop Pethick thinking that everyone wanted to break him. There were people in the factory who wanted to help him, and the only reason that nothing could be done, was because the factory itself was demolished. He had thought, too, it would be some comfort to Pethick to know he wasn't alone, that hundreds now were in the same boat that he was; and to hear also that Clyde had got his deserts. But Pethick was beyond such pleasures, and Barry felt ashamed. In the region where Pethick was now, these things made no difference that mattered.

'And the Time Study?' Ewa asked, in a low voice.

'Oh, that'll be all right, I'm sure,' said Mrs Pethick. 'Mr Spurrier always lands on his feet.'

They waited for him to go, they wanted only to be left. They had pulled together in a tight knot of love, and this love kept them and shut out everything else. Ewa was inside that knot, and sat there with the same locked intensity as her mother and father. They were like three views of one person. Barry looked at her helplessly, he could feel the desperate family love raging in the house like an electric storm, blasting, scarring. And she lived with them: in days, months, years, what would it do to her?

She was looking at him now. Her face was white, a queer hounded white face hanging in mid-air, gazing at him with a cut-off wistful hostility.

He knew why he had come, it wasn't for her father's sake, it was because of the way he froze when he heard her voice change on the phone, in the morning. It was too clear: the process he heard begin then was racing now to the end. He had studied time so long to no purpose, and now time pounced. If he were going to do anything, he must do it at once. There was no longer a kitchen or people there, but only the intense white tender-featured face, and the hostile wistful hungering eyes that went through him, reducing, transforming.

Abruptly he got up, and the stares of the three Pethicks swung upwards with him.

'Ewa, could I have a word? Do you mind?' Ewa sat paralysed, looking at the oddments on the table.

He must break the triangle they made. And Pethick, who hardly took in what he'd said about the factory, was alert at once to what he was doing now. In some way he was attacking the family. He got to his feet, meaning to throw Barry out: he had almost nothing now, he had only his family and he needed all of them. The brown wheels of his eyes stood out in his face, he looked at Barry with sheer hatred. Barry found he was trembling helplessly.

He said clearly, 'Ewa, please come.' By hook or by crook he would use the fact that he too was cut to the quick to get his own purchase on her. It would be a tale of woe: but it was only scaffolding, he would kick it away afterwards. But he felt weak as a baby. He waited, forcing the choice.

Ewa got up, without looking at Barry, and stood on her side of the table. Pethick glanced at her, and slowly sat back. Here too he was beaten, and, coming now, it was more cruel than anything else that had happened.

Ewa preceded Barry from the room, making it clear by her tense movements that she was going only to spare her parents the scene he was bent on making. They watched after her, not clear what had happened, but knowing they had had a defeat.

Presently they came back. Barry had said little, but he had planted his scaffolding and part of him was now in shock.

41

Petchey was tired and dazed, and didn't know whether he was awake or asleep. He thought he had got out of the factory, and broken into the old river country beyond the sandworks. In the hot silence he drifted through the trailers of willow. Then the river swung round, skirting a large hill, and such a terrible noise came from this hill that he was frightened to go near it. In spite of that he started clambering up between the close trunks—till the trees disappeared, and there was only a tract of bare mossy ground before he got to the top. The noise was very loud now, a clanging iron din. What had they got up there?

He laboured on, though the sky darkened and swooped over him. But now he stood on the crest and his sight cleared. Before him the hill slowly spread away in one deep sweet-smelling meadow of moist cool grass, deep-green and sweet like a pillowy sea. The railway engine, with its chain of clanking trucks, churned across the meadow. There were no tracks, but it steamed forward and the grass softly parted. All the men in the factory had their work-benches out in the field. Even the little canvas walls of the work-bays were set up like booths in the expanse of waving grass. The blacksmith had his anvil under a tree and swung his sledge there. As far as the eye could see, the field was dotted with men at benches, men shaking out drawings, chatting, smoking, carrying girders on their shoulders like stooks. The Drawing Stores was set down by itself, like a Punch and Judy stand, but someone else was inside it.

'What are you doing here?' he asked the plater beside him.

'It was too hot in the works,' the man explained, 'It was too hot by far.'

Petchey nodded.

Across the field sledge-hammers rose and fell, all the men were hammering.

'Join in, join in,' they sang, but when he tried to reply, the only sound he could make was a long groan.

'Join in, join in,' they said.

'I can't join in,' he cried, waving his right arm with the small black glove at the end.

He held up his dead right hand and stared at its square-sided iron shape. 'Come on, have a go,' the platers called, but he didn't listen. With his other hand, he started pulling off the black glove. As he peeled it back, his lightly haired wrist did not stop, but continued, widening. It was a strange sight because the black glove kept its small size as he pulled it off, yet inside there was a hand bigger than it. Mobile, ready, supple. He raised it and flexed his fingers, but he could scarcely see it, his eyes dazzled with wet light.

In his full eyes the trees and fields rippled like water, and as they rippled they went transparent, so that he glimpsed crammed shelves of drawings. Then he understood: the whole world was inside the Stores, the grass he stood on, the trees, the blue sky—they were all inside, and not only that, but the huge magnified box of the Stores was shrinking rapidly, so that on all sides the packed walls rushed towards him. The thought that he was inside the Stores again was more than he could bear, and out of him, or from somewhere, came a terrible long tearing shout. Then his sight went out, and he did not know where he was, but a deep pain at the base of his chest flared up and exploded, and he was only a tiny speck inside this pain. He heard himself snorting and gasping horribly, like a shot animal. Someone said, 'Is that a baby crying?' He scoffed, how could a baby get in the Stores? Then his hatred of the platers seized him like a sudden memory, it tightened through him and he strained to hold it down because it could kill him. But now he himself heard the shrill wailing cry of the baby, and he realized, it was the noise of a drill. But how odd, it sounded just like a baby crying. He seized on the cry and kept it sounding in his head, and the turmoil and fury and the ringing cry all quietened together, and he knew distinctly that someone there was going to die, and he felt so sorry, but who it was he didn't know, and the child's wail grew quieter and quieter and disappeared.

42

Eventually the large union meeting broke up, and the men moved uncertainly back to their workshops for what was left of the afternoon. And regular as clockwork, notwithstanding the crash, the thin, fair-haired pay-clerk, in his slender green-black suit, came round with a wooden tray rested on his hip, distributing small brown envelopes.

A number of platers resumed the job they had been doing: they wanted to finish it off. This presently brought a handful of men back to the Drawing Stores. They had forgotten all about Petchey.

'Len! Hey up, Len!' they shouted. There was no answer from the thick shutter, with its jagged yellow crack running from top to bottom.

They knocked on the hatch and rattled it, and shouted again.

'I'm getting a crow,' Trigg said, and he soon came back with one. He swung it into the hatch, then they all stood listening.

There was no outburst of rage from within.

Trigg swung the crow again and again, till he had made a large hole, jagged with splinters. He cautiously reached inside and unhooked the hatch. Then he banged it up, and fastened it.

Against the burning draught of stale air, he gingerly put his large head inside. Then, with much panting and squeezing, and some humorous assistance in the rear, he pulled the rest of himself after, and landed awkwardly in the Stores. He almost fainted, it was like landing in a furnace.

He looked round. The body of Len Petchey was awkwardly sprawled round the central column, but he could hardly see it at first because it was covered, as in a bed of fallen leaves, with small scraps of paper. The floor was littered with the chaotic bales of drawings that Len had at some stage snatched off the shelves, and on top of these was a thick layer of torn-up paper, it looked as though he had ripped a hundred drawings to shreds. The scraps were like a deep rich carpet on the floor, and they blew up through the Stores like leaves. Trigg made out among the tiniest shreds blue scraps and bits of Len's large commercial calendar.

43

The men didn't look round—the bush-telegraph ignored him completely—when, at the end of the afternoon, Clyde came out on his balcony. He stood there minutes in a dazed survey. With its weird trees and blocks of machinery, its concrete roads and steel peaks, the shop spread away like an iron city. He came down the stairs, to the soft clink of his iron, with a break and pause at each step. So he lost his large view of the shop. Up-ended drums and tall banks of machinery rose round him, and enclosed him when he stepped onto the floor.

His men were sprinkled among the machinery, in gangs and little knots, talking despondently. Near at hand, the florid charge-hand, Warboys, and the lanky plater, Bridger Jack, sat down on two toolboxes smoking. They sat towards each other, and looked as though they had paused for only a moment, while chatting. But the pause went on and on, while their quiet eyes gazed through the floor.

Clyde heard a violent rattle of voices, and saw, down the gangway, a batch of angry men waving their arms and shouting. The Shop Steward, Hawkins, was among them, hard-pressed and pleading. He kept running his fingers through his tangled hair, and talked on unheard while the men shouted.

Beyond them, a machine was working; it made an unfamiliar noise, with a regular beat and scrape, and Clyde tracked it to a small group of men at Jim Bundy's work-bay. Clyde went over, and stood at the back of the group.

Bundy had finished the conveyor now, and was showing it off. They all watched the thick belt sliding round the bank of rollers with a jerking rumble. Bundy, standing over the juddering machine with his arms akimbo, saw Clyde, and shouted over the rollers, his jutting face lit up, 'It works, Mr Clyde.' Clyde looked. As instructed, Bundy had let in a ratchet, so that each time the drive-wheel turned, only half of its turn actually pushed the conveyor belt forward: but when it did move, it moved at full speed. The machine was jerky, but it both did and didn't move at full speed in the way that was wanted, and the watching platers were so tickled by the ingenuity and simplicity together that they laughed with pleasure. They gathered round Clyde, and in the customary backhanded style of the shop, they congratulated him—with a certain reflected glory on the shop in general and the good men there. Clyde was so reduced now that at this tribute his eyes filled, and to hide them he had to scratch his brow non-stop.

He slipped away, and walked up the dead aisle between empty work-bays, idle machines, benches with tools and drawings neglected on them. He was wondering, would anything of his shop be left or remembered, or would all of it just disappear completely? He had always felt before that somehow everything the shop did fed and was part of the general modern surging progress of things. But now he knew that all of the shop would simply be wiped off the ground, nothing would be left, it need never have been. Yet the machines still existed, the thousands of machines they had made. They swarmed through the world. And on his own behalf, he thought: every so often a German or an Australian or a Peruvian would notice and appreciate one of the small inventions he had slipped into the mechanism. But then, who would notice these things when a new and better machine arrived? He saw a broad glittering army approaching, the legion of new machines that would supersede everything his shop had done. All their mixers and drills and plant would sooner or later be pushed into corners, dumped on scrap-heaps, left to the weather. The paint would blister and flake, and the exposed metal would mottle, scale, and crumble in the end to red dust. How many of their machines were already old corroding scrap? All his wonder was, how *could* he spend his life working, and never see it in this light? He wanted to say, it was all worthless, idiotic, it was all for nothing and he came out of it with nothing; yet still he couldn't say this. Was it only habit that stopped him? He turned and turned, at bay, striving in the dark.

He was half aware of the voices of George Reynolds and Jim Dawson, discussing with other men. There was argument, doubt, something was afoot. Presently men started to walk past him carrying hammers and sledge-hammers, crowbars, wrenches, old sections of pipe. They were massing at the end of the shop, armed with heavy steel. Then he remembered, he knew what they would do.

He glanced round, at a flicker of movement in the passage from the yard. Strudwick and Forbes had stopped on the threshold, watching in alarm as the men closed together at the far end. Clyde was tickled. What must they think?

Beyond the gathered men, Patrick Collier and George Reynolds got up on a bench, and, with more than the usual solemnity, Reynolds spoke a little, then handed a cardboard box to Collier. Collier was pleased and bashful. Not much was said, the occasion was muted and sad.

None the less, the platers now did what they always did when a man in the shop was going to be married. They took their hammers, crowbars, monkey-wrenches and pipes, and stationed themselves beside drums and guards, containers, girders, a half-completed hopper. At a slight movement from Reynolds, they touched the metal in front of them, and the entire shop vibrated to the low hum of reverberating steel. The hammers and crows knocked the iron again, and again harder, the new blows crashed on a strong booming that steadily grew louder. Presently the steel in the shop was not humming but roaring. All round the cones and drums and the hopper, bars and hammers rose and fell, out of rhythm, swiftly, it was a merciless battering, and the roar grew as though an ocean of sound were pouring into the shop and rising to the roof. Clyde glanced sideways, and saw plump Strudwick frozen with amazement, while pale Forbes looked on, shaking his head continuously. Each plater had his own time, and walloped as hard as he could on drums, bowls, hoods crammed solid with roaring echo. The ceremony had never happened on this scale, and Foreman Clyde, who usually stood by on such occasions, indulgent and fatherly, found a last use for the wrenches he carried in his pocket. He took out the largest and started hammering. The first blow sent a jagged hurt up his arm, as though the wrist-bone itself had hit the steel. He wasn't holding the wrench right, now he did, and hammered with all his strength.

Typists, clerks, even the time-studiers had come into the passage. The hammering put the Australian, Ted, into an ecstasy of amazement and exasperation, he rocked back and forth crying to Bert Cherry, 'Do you see what the silly buggers are doing! Christ, they're silly buggers here!' He was so full with indignant wonder he hugged himself and shook; while the blue clear forget-me-not eyes of Bert Cherry only widened more and more.

Platers who didn't like Collier, or hardly knew him, or whose marriages weren't at all of this tenor, hammered as though they hammered for life, their faces drawn, sweating, scowling with effort. Wilmot's mouth opened wide as he sang, at the top of his voice, inaudible. From the enormous incomplete hopper there came a deep pulsing throb, below all other sounds, like a great gong beaten continually, till from end to end the shop shivered and throbbed as though it were coming alive and had a beating iron heart that could finally be heard, deafening all other noise.

They had already gone on so much longer than usual that some of the platers looked round, alarmed, wondering when they would stop. But they did not stop, there was no slowing the momentum they had. Patrick Collier, whose wedding it was, looked on with a slow, bleak dawning in his face, a bitter knowledge was being hammered into his life. And the hammering went on as though it wouldn't stop until the doomed shop was already broken up and scattered in bits. Strudwick ran back and forth, frantic, ignored, able to do nothing, while great dents and scars developed in the battered iron. Clyde did not know where the fearful energy came from that kept him hammering till his arms burned with pain, and even so he only beat harder. Only, eventually, the hammering slackened; and quietened; and for a time the men hammered in a loosening chorus. Till the noise raggedly separated, and broke up in sporadic blows, and faltered to a ringing silence, crossed by distant sharp tappings and clashes of iron. The large doors at the end of the shop were open, and in a quiet completed excitement, talking quietly, the men all left the Plate Shop.